CW00507491

ELEPHANTS DON'T SNEEZE

A COLLECTION OF SHORT STORIES

PETER WYNN NORRIS

ISBN: 9781726791656

DEDICATIONS

The Barrack Road Writers in Northampton gave my writing a kick start and we could not have wished for a more able and dedicated tutor than Sally Spedding. She pointed me towards Maurice James's Coast to Coast Short Story Competition. My collection of stories is dedicated to Sally and to the memory of Maurice, who, sadly, is no longer with us.

Thank you to Ray Coles for the front cover picture.

CONTENTS

INTRODUCTION

I have written these short stories over the years. Some have been entries for national and international competitions, but most have been produced simply because the idea behind the story stirred up some deeper memories or just tickled my fancy. You may care to guess which is which!

Peter Wynn Norris August 2018

ELEPHANTS DON'T SNEEZE

Written in about 2003, this story was prompted by remarks from someone who worked at the type of school in this story. Also, children I knew were excluded from school on grounds that to me seemed questionable. Our education system at that time appeared to push every child through the same mould; children have different aptitudes and talents which often need different approaches to learning.

The end of a week that had been an emotional helter skelter ride. Jo Ford made the last round for the night. The dew on the tops of the twelve small tents glistened in the moonlight. These would be packed away when the Heathers school camp closed the next day. She savoured the stillness and even the country smells from the farm nearby. The old building of the Activity Centre looked dreamy in the moonlight. But now the reality jolt – twelve children, all classed as 'special needs', to be checked before she turned in for the night. A snuffle. A very faint snuffle, but there it was again. She went quietly to the nearest tent.

"Are you still awake, Jason, what's up?"

The sound of a sharp breathing in; a stifled sob.

She whispered, "Jason, what's up?"

Silence. Then more silence.

"Jason?"

She called his name louder as she opened the tent flap. The ten-year-old sat up, his sleeping bag clutched protectively round his neck. And then he started to talk. At first his voice was so quiet Jo couldn't make out what he was saying but she caught the word 'Rusty'.

"Who's Rusty, Jason?"

"Rusty's my dog."

His trickle of words burst into a gusher.

"It's time you were asleep," she said, when the boy was emptied of all the words he knew.

"I can't, Miss."

"I'll tell you a story to send you off."

"A what?"

How much disbelief was in those two words?

"Yes, a story. Just listen," and Jo started the only tale that came to her mind. How the elephant got its trunk. Kipling would have disowned it, but she told it the way her father had told it to her. The crocodile was finally defeated when the elephant sneezed and blew the reptile away for ever. Jason was asleep.

Thirty-five minutes later, Jo got back to the staff tents. Tony Mead, the only teacher on the trip, wiped his finger up the bottle of supermarket red, licking the drop of wine from it.

"I was just about to come and see where you were. What were you doing all that time? I didn't hear any rumpus. Any trouble?"

"Jason was brooding on something, so I told him a story. I thought the others were all asleep. Most weren't, and I had to tell each of them the same story."

Jo sat in a chair and sipped the drink.

"How was Jason?" asked Sue, Jo's fellow Classroom Assistant.

"He's on the brink. He was telling me about his dog,

Rusty. She's the only one he can talk to after he leaves us each day. He spends nearly all his time with her now. Sleeps in her basket, I shouldn't wonder."

Tony poured more wine.

"What was he worried about?"

"Rusty's having pups. His dad's girlfriend hates the dog – gets in the way of her – well, for want of a better word – clients. He just knows something will have happened to the dog while he's away."

They changed the subject. Tiredness and the strain of the week overtook them.

Bed.

The following morning the camp was over and getting through breakfast and cleaning up took longer than hoped but mercifully the thirty miles drive back through the countryside to the Heathers school was uneventful, with the boys hardly uttering a sound. Jason was particularly quiet, slumped in his seat, looking straight ahead. The minibus pulled onto the school's pitted tarmac drive as Alan Swift, the Head, walked down the steps.

"When you've put all the gear away, come in and tell me all about it," and he turned and went back into the building.

With the children gone, the three staff trooped into the Head's room. A tray of tea was ready on the table.

"As good as last year?" asked the Head.

Memories of the week were paraded. Once the banter and jokes were over, Jo felt troubled as she listened, as they moved into the war stories. There were not many positives being related. Things did go wrong when taking twelve 'special needs' children away on camp but there was always the likelihood of something good happening and they were the people who should recognise it. It was time to go home but something welled up inside her.

"We should be celebrating a good week, but we're not," she said, peering over her mug as though taking cover behind it.

"It was a *damned* good week for some of them."

She was nearly shouting.

"All we've just talked about is the way we've kept the lid held down. Take Jason. Before we went, no confidence, the others taking the mickey all the time or giving him a kicking even. During the week, he ran the legs off all of them in the orienteering, the only one to hit the target when they had a go at archery. Great at the weaving and the pottery. Imaginative. He listened and learned. By the end they were all looking up to him. '*How d'you do that Jason. Look what Jason can do, Miss.*' There are some good kids, given half a chance. By the end of the week they were like we never see them here. And now they go back to whatever passes for homes. What the hell are we doing? What is anyone doing?"

The mug had long been lowered to the table.

The Head made a steeple with his hands and looked away. Tony Mead was embarrassed by the outburst.

"This is the way it is, Jo, and there's little we can do to change it."

An embarrassed pause.

"Oh, let's get off home. I'm sure everyone's as tired as I am."

Tony delayed his going. The impression Jo made at the meeting was out of character. She was good to work with, a calming influence. Knowing Alan Swift's tendency for snap judgements, he felt compelled to put the record straight. He knocked on the Head's door and he pushed it open, as Swift slipped the bottle quickly into the bottom drawer. A glass with the two inches of clear liquid was still on the desk.

"End of a long hard week, Tony," said the Head, as he straightened up his tie. "Medicinal use only. Have one with me before we go home. Celebrate survival. That's the name of the game. Just between you and I that's what it's all about, isn't it?"

Tony was uncomfortable. It was as though he had caught one of the boys up to no good.

"Sorry, no, Alan. I only dropped in to see if you had any thoughts about what Jo had to say."

"Mrs. Ford? Got a bit emotional, didn't she? Still, she'll be OK by Monday. Bit of rest over the weekend."

"She did well at the camp. We could do with more like her."

No reaction from the Head.

"Anyway, I'm off. See you Monday."

As he shut the door Tony saw the glass lifted and the bottle being produced. Three years at the Heathers had been wearing. What would it be like after another three?

Monday morning. Jason had been on Jo's mind all weekend and now here he was coming through the school door. Normally he had nothing to say until half way through the day but now there was obviously something waiting to burst out, and it came in a rush.

"I'll kill him, Miss."

Jo looked at him.

"They're strong words, Jason. Who are you going to kill?"

"My dad."

A long pause.

"My dad's a bastard."

Jo had to bend lower to see Jason's face.

"If you want, we'll talk about this once assembly is over."

Jason stood, still rigid, still staring at his feet.

"Would you like that?"

"Yeah."

He walked into the school. Then he turned, nodding his head rapidly.

"Yeah," he said with more conviction.

With assembly over, Jo followed the small group of boys into the classroom. How many this morning? She counted. There should be twelve but so far there were only nine. One was in court and two Heaven knows where. Better than most mornings though.

The teacher stood by his table at the front of the room. He watched the boys as they went to their desks.

"Tony, a quick one, please. I need to have a talk with Jason as soon as possible."

The teacher turned to the Classroom Assistant.

"Jo, we're far enough behind with the curriculum as it is and with OFSTED almost on us. Can't it wait?"

She wanted to scream out, *you insensitive clod*, but what

came out was, "No it can't. Come on Jason,' and they both went off to a quiet room.

Jason sat for minutes without speaking and then it poured out.

"He's done it Miss. He's killed Rusty and her pups. Five. He told me they had gone to be looked after. Saturday Wayne showed me them in a skip down the street."

Now the tears were a flood. Jason's body heaved with the sobbing. Jo hugged the thin body and the boy clung to her, his whole being stiffened. Jo felt the watering in her own eyes.

"Stay here Jason and I'll get you a drink."

She brought the drink and then went to see the Head.

"Yes, it is a problem. But don't forget that he was excluded from two schools. You probably know him better than I do, but you must admit he can be a handful. Didn't he assault you once?"

Jo opened her mouth to speak but the Head continued, "He can't remain here today in his present state and we can't send him home. I need to bring the Social Services in," and he was on the phone as Jo returned to her classroom.

Two hours later she saw Jason leaving the Heathers with a social worker. She tried to clear her mind of the boy and his troubles. With Social Services taking him, he should be in safe hands. She immersed herself in whatever needed doing.

A week passed and Jason had not been seen at the school. This caused no concern since they would be told whether he was going to return and if not what else would happen to him. Jo asked around about him but there was no information. Sue was the first with the news at coffee break on Thursday.

"I was talking to a neighbour who works at the hospital. She asked me if a lad named Jason Warmby was one of ours and I said, 'probably, why?' And she said he was admitted last week. He'd had a beating. The police had been called and they said his dad had laid about him with a baseball bat."

The feelings as she hugged the boy the last time she had seen him returned to swamp Jo.

"Is he still in the hospital?"

"I don't know, but I've got a few minutes, so I'll phone."

Sue discovered that Jason had been discharged a few days before, but she could find out no more. After school that afternoon, Jo went to the Hospital. Jason had been discharged into the care of the Social Services. More phone calls.

"They told me that Jason's in the Local Authority children's home," she explained to Sue. "That's probably for the best. He'll be out of his father's range. He won't be coming back to the Heathers now."

It jolted her when Alan Swift put his head into the classroom and signalled for her to come out.

"Someone here wants to see you, Mrs. Ford. Let's go to my room."

The police constable sat fingering the hat in his hands.

"Jason Warmby, Mrs. Ford. He asked me to see you."

"What's all this about? What's he done now?"

"It's not what *he's* done. You know he went to the Children's Home? Well, the evening he went in, two girls set about him. It's said it was because he wouldn't smoke weed with them. They did him up badly. Ruptured spleen the worst part."

The policeman looked straight at Jo as if weighing up how to continue.

"He insisted there was something you had to know." The constable shuffled his feet. "Sounded a bit daft to me."

"Go on."

"He said to tell you, 'Elephants don't sneeze.'"

Jo felt her heart leap. She smiled. The last night of camp, the moonlight, the tents, the farmyard smells.

"Of course I know what it means! Fancy him remembering that. I must go and see him."

"I'm afraid you can't."

Jo bristled. "I don't see that you can stop me."

"He died last night."

To the constable, it seemed Jo would never move and then she raised her head and sobbed, "He was a sweet kid really."

"What did you say?" said the constable.

GOODBYE DOLLY GRAY

The title of this story is the name of a song from Boer War times and rejuvenated during the 1914-18 war. Alfred Marks singing this in the Old Time Music Hall on TV made an impression on me. This, plus occasional conversations with my father who served throughout the 1914-18 war, fuelled this story.

What do you want Mum? Muu-um? I didn't go into Twitter, Snapchat or whatever, honest. Would I come and tell you about it if I had? Well, would I? You've told me to keep off those social media... That's what they call them, Mum. Anyway, I don't even know how to get into them. I know you don't believe it but I was looking for something to help me with my project on WWI. *What's WWI?* Really, Mum, World War One, of course. And I wouldn't go to Twitter for that, would I?

I'd just put 'WWI' into the Internet and then up on the screen came the words, *What are you looking for Daniel?* Yeah, really. Just like that. No, I don't know what brought it up on the screen but it looked good, so I typed in, *Help with my project.* And he says... *How do I know it was a 'he'?* Because he told me his name later. No of course I hadn't told him mine, I never let on who I am, like you told me, but he knew my name anyway. Look, Mum, do you want to know about this or what? Good, well let me carry on, will you?

He says, *Well maybe I can help you with that.* And I say, *How?*

and he says, *You'll see, but first let's have a bit of what the froggies call a parlee view.* Yes, that's exactly how it came up on the screen and I said, *What's that mean?* and he said, *That's French for a bit of a chat.* So I said, *Chat about what?* and he said, *About who's in your family. Who are they and what are they called?* And I told him, *Dad, who's called Mister Harold Gray and everyone calls him Harry,* and then about you, Mum, and Sarah. And do you know what he said? He said, *I'm glad to know the good old names are still there.* Yes, Mum, I know it sounds as if he was getting too personal, but I couldn't stop him saying it, could I, short of switching off and I didn't want to do that. So I said, *What do you mean?* He said, *Everyone knows there's always been a Harry and a Sarah in the Gray family. And a Dan too, most times.* That's exactly what he said, Mum. I wrote it down. Do you know what he was getting at? Yes I suppose Dad might. I'll ask him when he comes home.

Did he help me with my project? You still don't believe me, do you? I was coming to that. He said, *What sort of things do you want to know about the Great War?* That what he called it, the Great War and I'd never heard it called that before, only WWI. I said our teacher had told us that we had to get beyond just the facts and find out what it really felt like, you know, in the trenches and out of them too. And then he asked me a funny question. *What are you having for tea?* and I said I had got my favourite strawberry jam sandwiches with me by the computer. He said, *that's what they had in the trenches,* though they weren't nice little sandwiches like I would have. They had bread door steps and *'pozzy'* - that's what he said they called strawberry jam. It came in ten-pound tins. And he asked, was I having any gunfire? I said I didn't know what he meant and he said, *don't they teach you anything these days. Tea, Dan boy*, he said. *Tea.* Gunfire was what they called it. *Sergeant Major's, strong enough to stand your spoon up in it,* he said. And they had hard tack and bully beef all the time until they were sick of it. *But it was food.*

How do you think he knew all this, Mum? I know, just know he wasn't having me on because then he said – yes, he **said**, it was his voice, not writing on the screen any more – "You wanted to know what it *felt* like to be there. See what you make of this, Dan lad. Put yourself in your Uncle Arthur's place. You have heard of your uncle Arthur, haven't you?"

And I said, no, I hadn't.

And he said, "Well, he joined up in 1915. Told them he was eighteen, but he was really only seventeen. Lots of young men did that. Go and fight for King and Country, they were told."

Mum, that's only as old as Michael next door. I couldn't see him fighting in the army, could you? Uncle Arthur – he said he would have been my great great great Uncle, but I don't know how he worked that out – was at Wipers when some of his mates and the mule carrying their machine gun were blown off the duckboard in front of him by a 'whizzbang'. That was a specially loud German shell meant to frighten. He said that the crater was mud, no bottom to it or so it seemed, and Uncle Arthur never saw them or the mule again.

"Now," he said, "how do you think Arthur felt,

standing there on that duckboard? The men all came from this town, his town, some even from his own street."

I said I felt sick when he told me that and he said, "Well you would, wouldn't you? Arthur never recovered. Shell-shock they called it, though he nearly got shot for a coward."

Mum, it was as though I was right there. There was something about his voice. What's that? Yes, there some more.

"What about the womenfolk, then, young Daniel?" he said. "I'll bet you haven't thought about that. Take your great great Grandma, Edie Gray. She left school at 12 and went to work in the paper mills. That was well before the war. Come 1914 they turned the mills over to munitions and that's what the women did, made munitions, rifle bullets, shells, grenades and so on"

Did you know we had a great great grandma Edie, Mum? I've never heard of her. Yeah, I'll ask Dad about her too. He went on about her. Said she was really good at doing sums in her head. She was eighteen when the war started and she joined the Wax. I said, what was that and he said, the Women's Auxiliary Army Corps. She was good at organising things and by 1915 she was in charge of a camp kitchen at a barracks in Surrey, cooking for the Cannucks. Yeah, that's what he called them. Canadians, I think. He said he remembers reading her Army cookery book, *Beef and Onion Stew with Dumplings. Take one side of beef, two hundredweight of potatoes, two stones of onions...* And so on. Bit different to your cooking Mum – *Take one pack of frozen fish fingers and one tin of mushy peas* – yeah, alright I am cheeky.

And then he said he thought that was enough to be getting on with. If I wanted to know any more, to put his name into the computer and it would find him.

I said, "But I don't know your name," and he said, "Lord love us, lad, same as yours of course, Gray. The first name's Robert. They always called me Dolly though. You know how it is in the army, all Whites are Chalky, Murphys are Spud, Millers are Dusty and all Grays are Dolly."

I get the Whites, Murphys and Millers but Grays being called Dolly doesn't make sense, I said.

"Haven't you ever heard that song 'Goodbye Dolly Gray'? Everyone was singing it. I used to sing it to Edie."

And you won't believe this Mum, I hadn't got the speakers switched on, but his voice came out through them singing, *"Goodbye Dolly I must leave you, though it breaks my heart to go."*

I can't remember the lot, but a bit of it stuck in my mind.

"Hark I hear the bugles calling …good bye Dolly Gray."

And when he finished the song he said, "Don't forget, look me up."

Yes I have, Mum. At first I was scared to but here's what I found on the War Memorial web site. I wrote it down. *GRAY, Sergeant Robert, 1st Bedfordshire and Hertfordshire Regiment of Charles Street.* That's only down the hill off Kings Road. *Age 25. Son of Daniel and Sarah.* Daniel. He said there's always been a Daniel in the family. *Killed in action on*

18

1st August 1918. Ypres (Menin Gate) Memorial. Formerly employed at the town Gas Company and a member of the St. Peter's Town Band. Father of Daniel born July 1918. It's really wicked… It's all there. It couldn't have been him really talking to me, could it, Mum? Could it? Really could it? I don't know if I want to go on the computer again.

2.04 a.m. said the red numbers on the bedside clock radio. It was faint, but he could hear the voice. It was his. Dolly Gray's. It was clear and it wasn't in his bedroom. It had to be coming from downstairs. He pulled back the duvet, put his feet on the floor and listened again. He didn't want to put the light on. He blundered against the dressing table as he made for the door.

His mother and father heard him moving.

"That's Dan. He's up and about," said his mother.

"What are you doing Dan?" called his father.

"Can't you hear him, Dad?"

Dan was three steps down now, standing, peering into the darkness that was the downstairs, listening. He was scared but he had to go on.

"I've got to go and see him. I've got to find out."

"Harry, he was killed, for Heavens sake. We don't know how was he killed. What state is he in now?"

His mother was sobbing.

"Stop him, Harry; he mustn't see him, stop him."

Dan was now at the bottom of the stairs. The voice was clear and it came from the sitting room. He stood and listened. He hadn't turned the lights on. Was there really anyone there? Dare he go in? And then the voice spoke.

19

"You came down, then. You're a good 'un, young Daniel. I'm so glad you did. I needed the company."

His father flicked the light switch in the hall and his hand caught Daniel by the shoulder.

"It's imagination, Dan. Come on back to bed. It's all imagination you know. You've a big day at school tomorrow."

His father's hand was hurting as it steered him back to the stairs. From behind the closed door of the sitting room Dan heard the voice once more.

"Feel I'm home again. Come and see me. We've a lot to talk about. I shan't go away."

The singing started, "Hark I hear the bugle calling. Good bye Dolly Gray."

BLUES FOR BRONWEN

I was looking for a used soprano saxophone. I came across a varied range of instruments in pawn shops and, from the look of some of them, there was no telling where they had been. All sorts of ideas emerged, and the story pushes on from there.

The rain came down like shotgun pellets. I ducked into this Cash Exchanger just off the city centre and it wasn't just to get out of the rain. Something steered me into the shop. Everything was crammed together, fishing rods, cabinets filled with cameras, and the like.

"What the hell am I doing here?" I kept muttering, but now I was being drawn inexorably to the soprano saxophone which was standing at the end of the shelf, a yard of straight metal tube, with a mouthpiece at one end and a bell at the other.

It was in good nick, but someone had knackered a key pivot and the repair had left a sharp edge. The instrument was ugly, and yet something compelled me to want it. I've always been sniffy about soprano saxes, so why was I in a pawn shop trying out this bizarre bit of metal ware? After I had played a few arpeggios I had the strangest feeling. The instrument was moving my fingers, not the other way round.

By the way, I'm Lol Longwith, and I play clarinet in a London band and we'd been playing gigs in Wales. I jumped ship in Cardiff to follow the lovely Glynis home. It didn't work out.

But back to what I was saying. I paid up and then cursed myself for buying the saxophone, but now I was home and could give it a real blow. Try as I might to do 'Georgia', I was playing something I'd never heard before. I tried again, but I was off into another tune I didn't know. I was confused. I wiped the instrument and put it away.

The band is Josh Cato's Hot Cats, Dixieland, and we earn our crust playing anywhere that will pay enough. HQ is a pub in Tottenham. I went round there at the usual rehearsal time.

"So, you got back, then. I was thinking about getting another clarinet, man."

I'd heard our leader blew a fuse when I didn't appear, but now he was all smiles because he had landed a series of dates with one of the holiday hotel chains. We ran over the new tunes and he gave the thumbs up. The rest of the band had drifted off to the lounge bar, but Josh was still there.

"What's on your mind, Lol?"

"I'd like to give my soprano a go in the band."

"Forget it. No soprano in my band. It'll upset the balance."

He turned, shook the spit out of his trumpet and packed it away.

The next gig was at Lowestoft, a big one – audience of six hundred guaranteed. I was in my flat waiting to be picked up, when the doorbell rang. I grabbed my bag and clarinet case, and I caught a glimpse of the soprano. I swear it was winking at me. I closed the lid of its case and slipped in under my coat.

We arrived with just enough time to get on stage. Josh bounced on like a rubber ball and raised his arms to the audience.

"Here we go with that good old stomper, 'Dinah'."

His foot stamped out the tempo and we were off. We went through the first set, tramping away like mad. We came to the end, Josh blew kisses to the audience, and it was change over time. Another hour before we were on again.

Our final set was going well. Eleven-forty-five, there was still a large crowd and Josh was riding high. My clarinet was on its stand and I was clapping out the rhythm, getting the punters going. Josh was carried away and into his third chorus of 'Margie'. He was rocking and swaying, and his foot caught his mike stand. The mike went flying and landed on my clarinet. Talk about fate! All that happened later can be traced to this moment. I hadn't put the mouthpiece cap on. I ran my thumb along the black ebonite of the mouthpiece. I felt the roughness and my stomach turned over. The slightest chip on the business surfaces of a clarinet mouthpiece and the thing is knackered. Useless.

I nipped behind the back curtain and dug out the soprano. I blew heavily through the instrument to warm it up and was back in time to round the number off. Josh was getting a great hand and looked as though he hadn't noticed anything. Next number. I could feel the soprano working on my hands. It wanted to go faster than I was playing and I couldn't hold it in check. Josh looked sideways at me, his lips drawn back, and not just to blow his trumpet. I was into 'Honeysuckle Rose' they told me later. I only know I was blowing like fury.

It was over. The sweat dripped off me. The applause was a spontaneous roar. "More, more, more!" rang out across the room. Josh was looking daggers at me, cursing like a jazzman who has been asked to play 'Happy Birthday' for the fifth time that evening. Then the very last number, the last of the whole weekend.

"Here we go then, big finale. 'Summertime'. Lol, *Summer Bloody Time*. One two, one, two three four," and he pounded the tempo with his foot.

Josh was stating the melody like a good trumpet should, but then the metal in my hands began to pulse. It was tugging my fingers, not the other way round. My instrument was up and I was blowing, blowing like a November gale. And then I realised I was well into 'Wildcat Blues'. 'Summertime' had gone by the board. I'd never played like this before. It was ecstasy. It came so easily and I blew and blew, the soprano pointing at the ceiling, my back arched as I thrust myself into the music. It was, well… climactic.

Josh muttered a farewell into the mike and as we reached the band room, he grabbed my shirt front and pulled my face close to his.

"What the hell do you think you were doing? You changed the tune and hogged the limelight. I've told you before, *no* soprano. Whose band is this?"

His neck was bulging and the vein on the side of his temple stood out, throbbing. Our trombone player, Dave, pushed between us.

"You've got a point, Josh, but just listen to that audience. They're still raving. We've never, ever, done one like that."

Dave motioned to me to get out of it as he took Josh by the shoulder and steered him away.

I went to the Wagon and Horses on the Monday with some trepidation. I was the last to arrive and was surprised to find Josh missing. Dave was in the leader's chair.

"Josh's got a slipped disc or something. Bill Filkins is standing in for him. Our next date is in that castle in North Wales," and he turned to me. "Without Josh, we'll need to beef things up. I want you to do some numbers on the soprano. I'll take the flak from Josh later. What'll you play?"

He was astonished when I said, "I won't know what to play until I start."

Dave raised his eyes to the heavens.

"God help us! We won't know the key or anything!"

Eiffon, our drummer, produced the answer.

"Lol starts. I back him for a few bars. Then you come in. We should know the chords by then."

Dave pondered. "It might work."

And up in Wales it did work. Our first set was trudging along more like a 1920s dance orchestra than a Dixieland band and then, fifteen minutes before the end, I lifted the soprano. I can honestly say I didn't know what tune I was playing. It was only after several bars that I realised I was into 'Ain't Misbehaving'. Eiffon had stayed with me and the two of us cruised on together. Dave and Bill jammed away on their horns. The band had never sounded better. Our second set followed the same pattern. The dancers stopped their gyrations to listen and the applause rose to a crescendo.

Back at the flat on Tuesday I got my usual paper and happened upon Justin Whelk's music column. Justin is a jazz man too. His Bessie Smith 'sound alike' has been around for ever.

> Sunday night was more than a revival. It saw the rebirth of Sidney Bechet. And if you don't know who Bechet was, you ought to be ashamed. He was almost as great a force in the jazz world as Louis Armstrong. Lol Longwith not only played Bechet, he was Bechet. A bunch of tunes from the master's French period not only had the notes but all the passion that was Bechet's hallmark. If you have the slightest interest in music, look out for Lol Longwith.

Two days later Eiffon came round to my flat.

"I found it a bit hard to swallow when you said you didn't know what you were going to play. I've done some research. The tunes you played at the last gig were the ones Bechet recorded in Paris shortly before he died. They were never released."

"Well?"

Slowly and in low tones, he said, "I believe your soprano is possessed by the spirit of the great man."

I laughed. Haunted houses, crypts, and old abbeys but never a haunted saxophone.

"Even for a mystic from Maesteg, that's going a bit far. You mean, it wasn't me who was actually playing? Pull the other one."

"Humour me, Lol. There's someone who knows about these things. Will you see her?"

"I'll bet she's from Wales, too."

"As a matter of fact, she is. She's my Auntie Bronwen."

I was so curious now, that I agreed and Eiffon said he would bring her round the next day. I'd recently seen 'Blithe Spirit' on tele and I fully expected a Madame Arcati type. Eiffon is in his thirties and amazingly his aunt wasn't much older. She had gorgeous red hair shaped round her face. Her slim figure needed no flattering from the clothes she wore, but the emerald of her sweater picked out the green in her eyes. I brought the sax through from the bedroom. It looked lifeless, sullen almost. Bronwen took a crystal pendulum on a light silver chain from her bag.

"What I am going to do is dowse to find out if there is a presence in the saxophone," she announced, taking the pendulum.

I must have sniggered.

Those green eyes pierced me. "The presence of sceptics can stop the dowsing working."

I didn't want her walking out in a huff or walking out at all. I said, "Bronwen, I really want to get to the bottom of this."

"The pendulum can say 'yes' or 'no'. Look. If it spins clockwise it's saying 'yes'. Anti-clockwise it means 'no'. It all depends upon the questions I ask."

She looked at the soprano.

"Did Lol buy you in Cardiff?"

A 'yes' from the pendulum. She nodded and asked more questions getting 'yes' or 'no' answers.

"Now comes the interesting bit," and her eyes were widening.

She looked at the instrument and asked in a low voice, "Is there a presence inside you?"

I fought hard to hold back the giggle but the pendulum went ballistic – a definite 'yes' – and she looked at the horn.

"Were you a musician?"

Clockwise once more. She produced a pad with the letters of the alphabet in a circle round it.

"I want you to spell your name."

She used a pointer to indicate the letters, one by one. The pendulum started to rotate as she reached the letter G. She continued until she had the letters G O M.

"It's a strange name, but it's all I can get. Does that mean anything, boys?"

"Nothing," Eiffon and I said in concert.

We were deflated. One moment we were steaming along a track of excitement and now we had hit the buffers.

Bronwen walked back to Eiffon's digs with her nephew and I managed to tag along. I have to admit I was besotted with her.

Josh hadn't been seen lately, but we heard he was still unable to travel. We had another hotel date and I did some Bechet numbers again, or rather the soprano did. The same rapturous applause. The next Monday we all met and were standing around with our instruments.

"What a weekend session!" Dave was saying. "Josh Cato's Hot Cats are on a roll and it's all due to Lol here."

And then a familiar voice boomed out. "Except it's not Cato's Cats any more. It's Longwith's bloody tin whistlers."

Josh had come in by the side door. He smelt of whisky.

"You cut me out while I was sick."

Josh staggered to my side and with deceptive speed whipped the soprano from my hand and crashed it down on my forehead. The key that had been mended was sharp and bit in deeply. I dropped.

*　　*　　*

The funeral was in the jazz tradition – a parade along the streets to the crem – playing 'Oh Didn't He Ramble' and 'Just a Closer Walk with Thee.' Afterwards they all went back to the Wagon for a jam session. Eiffon had put the soprano on the coffin along with my clarinet but someone had brought the soprano back to the pub.

After the inquest, Josh was prosecuted for manslaughter, convicted and got a community service order. A few months went by and I found myself travelling. Cardiff this time. The applause was fantastic. Justin Whelk's column said it all:

Not since the untimely death of Lol Longwith have we heard playing like this. Miraculously, Sidney Bechet yet again came to life in Cardiff in the person of a ravishing red-head, Bronwen Williams. No-one in the jazz world has heard of her, but what a recipe for success — beauty and the beast of an instrument.

Whelk reported all Bronwen's concerts enthusiastically. And then came true recognition – an invitation to play at the Barbican. There was excitement as she walked onto the stage, her red hair a beacon of fire and her long, tight evening gown emphasising her figure. She brought the soprano to her lips and she blew. And what came out wasn't the vibrato rich music of Bechet. Just a reedy screech. She tried again; the same result and Bronwen fled the stage.

*　　*　　*

In the quiet of the nursing home, Bronwen held the saxophone in her hands. The breakdown had done nothing to blemish her looks and she was as lovely as ever, but her voice cracked as she said, "You can't stay in there, Lol. It's time you moved on."

I weighed up what she was saying and concluded this was one of those times to materialise.

"We're sorry we didn't blow for you at the Barbican, but I don't want to move, Bronwen. As long as you are running your fingers up and down the soprano I'm happy where I am. By the way, G O M. wasn't someone's name. G.O.M. stood for *Grand Old Man*. Sidney tells me that's what they used to call him. He couldn't resist a little joke since you looked so serious. We've agreed to take it in turns to do the playing from now on."

It truly was a horn of plenty.

FACING THE MOUNTAINS OF THE MOON

The state of up-country roads, the ferocity of some storms, and a poliomyelitis epidemic in Uganda were the foundations for this story. The Mountains in question are the Ruwenzori, which formed a barrier between Uganda and the then Belgian Congo. More romantically they were also known as the Mountains of the Moon.

An afternoon in February 1952

The sky had been heavy with rain clouds since early morning. These slate grey monsters of the air held back their water, their thousands of gallons of water ready to slop earthwards the second they felt the urge. The clouds grumbled to each other without stop.

Behind them were the mountains, the fabled Mountains of the Moon. The clouds settled over the heights like a sodden grey blanket. Below them in the foothills lay the township, a dozen Asian shops, a cluster of government offices, police station and hospital, and houses for the small European and Indian population. The hospital had been planned for local African population and its facilities could never quite cope with the demands placed on it.

At four thirty in the afternoon, it was dark enough for the oil lamps. Hamish Boyd, District Medical Officer, strode down the red earth path to the last of the European bungalows. He kept looking up at the clouds, their malevolence oppressing him. He rapped on the door and entered. She stood to the right as he walked in. The doctor nodded to the woman on the verandah and strode on further into the house. His eyes and nose smarted from the strength of the disinfectant, liberally used all through the house.

No one had attended to the lamps here. The nursing sister's white uniform glowed in the gloomy interior where the heavy wooden government issue furniture was just discernible.

The medical man went through to the bedroom to the long figure motionless on the bed. He shone a small torch into the pupils of the patient's eyes. sounded the chest and checked the pulse. He shook his head, folded the stethoscope and moved through to the lounge. The woman stood alongside the nurse.

"We've got to get him to Kampala. They've got the facilities there. I've phoned to make the arrangements."

He looked at the woman whose husband was lying in the bedroom.

"It's going to be a long drive. You can come in my car."

He nodded towards the nurse, "Jane will be in the Land Rover with your husband."

He moved to the front door and looked up at the sky.

"I'd have liked to have been off an hour or two ago, but the Land Rover was still out. With a bit of luck it won't rain. It's held off all day."

The telephone rang. The doctor answered it and as he returned it to its cradle he announced, "The driver's fuelling up the Land Rover now. Are you ready? Is the emergency bag packed? I'll go and get my car. I'll only be five minutes."

It took the combined strength of all of them to manoeuvre the awkward shape of the patient on the rigid stretcher from the bedroom, out down the six wooden steps to the long wheel-base Land Rover. From the passenger seat, the nurse would be able to see the patient's head as he lay in the rear of the vehicle.

The two vehicles left the township's edge. The Land Rover led, travelling gingerly at first. Driver Okech knew from long experience that forty-five miles per hour was the right speed for the vehicle to skip along the tops of the washboard corrugations of the red gravel. Okech knew his passenger was very ill, but this was not any passenger, this was his OC, Mr Barker.

The doctor's Citroen Light Fifteen followed far enough behind to avoid the plume of red dust thrown up. Mile forty-five now, and they were passing the clearing where stood the rondavels of the road gang of the Public Works Department.

"Less than a hundred miles to go. We're making excellent progress. Okech is a good driver. None better." He said this as much for his own comfort as for the passenger beside him.

Are clouds capable of playing tricks? Dirty, malicious tricks? Are they like snakes? Few attack without cause, but some do. Fanciful, maybe, but on this day, at this time, the wind had risen and the clouds stirred, celestial bulk carrying craft, slopping with water to pitch to the earth below. As the wind grew stronger, they sailed the quicker. They overtook the two vehicles and they held their loads no longer. The wind compressed the heavy drops of rain into a sheet that swept along the road's surface.

The PWD road gang had finished their work that afternoon. Whether it was idleness or the lack of the correct materials, who knows, but they had filled the deep ruts and cavernous wash-aways from earlier rain with black cotton soil. The approved road mending material was red laterite that should have been sieved and compacted into the road's surface.

Driver Okech peered through the windshield of his Land Rover. He squinted to get a better view, but nothing he could do improved the visibility. The wipers would just not clear the glass quickly enough. Even with all his experience he was not ready for the sideways slide that pointed the vehicle at the very edge of the road. He slammed hard on the four-wheel drive knob and engaged the transfer box, doubling the power of the gears. The Land Rover rolled, slid, crabbed its way backwards through the black slush.

The Citroen had stopped before the mud slick.

"What's happening?" asked his passenger.

"I can't see too well."

Boyd wound his window down. His head and shoulders were soaked.

"Okech has spun but he's OK now. We'll wait here for a bit to see what happens."

"Will he be alright?"

"Of course. Don't worry."

Jane let go of the grab bar in front of her. She watched as the wheel whipped to and fro in Okech's hands, moved by the elements rather than by the driver. The vehicle steadied. She turned and looked at her patient by the light of her torch, stretched and managed to place her fingers on Mike Barker's carotid artery. There was still a pulse, though faint. How much do you know, Elaine, sitting back there in the doctor's car?

"They're moving forward again," said the MO. "Yes, they're on their way again."

He couldn't see that the clouds had brought up their reserves. Heavier, more laden with water than those before them, the earlier downpour was as nothing to the cascade now.

Okech felt the wheels grip. They were still moving straight ahead, twirling the gooey mixture that should have been firm earth had PWD done their job properly. *And* there hadn't been this rain.

"We're still moving, memsahib." Reassurance, a message of comfort for Jane.

"I think he's through the worst, Elaine," and the doctor started the Citroen ready to move forward from the red laterite to the rain-washed earth that shone like a black river under the car's headlights.

"Oh, my God. They've hit a wash-away."

The MO saw the Land Rover jerk and tilt, the angle so steep, he held his breath until he was forced to gasp.

"What's happening. I can't see?"

The woman sat gripping her seat as she watched the vehicle carrying her husband sink deeper into the morass before her eyes.

"I'll go and find out."

The doctor opened his door and winced as he saw the depth of the mud and felt the rain. He couldn't hold back now, however much his inclinations said, stay where you are. He felt around for his bag, braced himself to set off. The sticky porridge came over the top of his shoe and oozed down into his sock. His other foot hovered and then he thrust it down and forced himself towards the Land Rover. Now his only concern was to keep his balance, not to slip head first into the mud.

Blood oozed from Okech's forehead where it had banged against the dashboard. He righted his round khaki pillbox hat and tried to start the stalled engine. It ground and moaned and ground again. The carburettor was flooded and he knew there was nothing he could do but wait until the vehicle, in its own good time, consented to start. Jane managed to turn her torch onto the patient's face despite the awkward angle, but she couldn't reach to touch him. What was his condition now? She didn't know. The hammering on the door startled her. She could only see the face peering in. The door was pulled open and she moved towards Okech to make room for the doctor.

"Are you all right? Good. How's Mike? Silly question, really. What can we say about a polio patient in the dark, in a storm, miles from anywhere from help."

Despite his despondency, he went round to the back of the Land Rover. He lowered the tailgate and scrambled up into the vehicle His examination was brief. Torch. Stethoscope. No more.

"There's still life in him," he announced, as he pushed his head through the gap in the canvas that separated the cab from the body of the vehicle. Jane nodded but her lip trembled. Driver Okech turned and spoke in Swahili.

The doctor asked, "What's he say, Jane?"

"He says there is a cotton ginnery a mile or so down the road. He is going to walk there and get help."

The driver pulled on his raincoat and neither of the Europeans saw his going once he had moved from the vehicle.

"I'll go back to my car and wait there. Will you be all right here?"

"I'll be just fine."

Will I really? So close to Mike and so far.

As the medical officer lowered himself into the seat of his car his passenger stirred. She spoke.

"He's all right now, Hamish? He's resting, isn't he?"

The doctor inclined his head to her and said, "That's right, Elaine," and switched the light off. It would be easier if he couldn't see her face.

She continued, "I shouldn't want anything to go wrong. We go on UK leave next month, and he has to be fit for that." Her voice lifted. "Mike's got a trial with Wakefield Trinity, you know. Rugby League. Semi professional. Mike was with the East African XV that toured the Copperbelt. They must have thought he was good as someone wrote straight off to Wakefield."

"I saw him play in Kampala. He *was* good, very good…"

He checked himself. Joining in her game won't help

her.

'Elaine, listen…" But she wasn't listening.

"They say you can earn good money playing Rugby League. Then we can stay in the UK. I've had enough of Africa."

Jane Cartwright felt the hardness of the Land Rover's seat. She was alone and isolated. What do you do on a dark stormy night in your own sea of mud? There's not much else to do but think. And Jane, you keep coming back to the same thoughts. You're not alone, are you? Mike's here with you. On another occasion what wouldn't you have given to be alone in a car at night with him? But not like this. He's ill and you're useless. There's nothing you can do for him. You're sitting here useless and he's the only man you've ever cared for. Loved, whatever that might mean. And his wife is sitting forty yards away. Who are you? Jane Cartwright. Plain Jane, spinster of the parish. Thirty-five, unmarried.

She lifted her head and shouted aloud, "For God's sake, Okech, come back with some help and get us out of here. I can't stand my own company any longer."

The light of the vehicle coming towards her answered her appeal and lifted her solitude. She felt shame, though she didn't know why. She could see Driver Okech struggling forward with a tow rope. He slid down the hole in front of the Land Rover and then he was climbing into his rightful position behind his own vehicle's steering wheel. He pressed the starter. The engine whirred, coughed, spluttered, coughed again and fired. He revved and the engine stammered and burst into song. Jane could have sung with it. She could see the tow rope tighten. So tight now, that its tension flicked droplets of mud into the air, sparkling in the headlamp glare.

Hamish Boyd sat watching. The rain had stopped and his windshield was clear. The Land Rover, forty yards in front of him, was moving. Its passage was rough but it was moving. The rear end was now down in the hole and the front was rising, all in slow motion. Yes, now it was on an even keel, moving through the mud more easily. He started his own engine. He knew the front wheel drive of the Citroen could handle almost any road and he drove slowly into the black cotton soil. He could see the way ahead now. He forced his eyes away from the deep hole to his right where the Land Rover had nearly met disaster and fixed them on that bit of road that was left to him. He stopped and wound his window down. An Indian dressed in a white shirt, with an ill-fitting waistcoat and dhoti came over to him. It was Maganbhai Patel, the ginnery owner.

"Ah, doctor, I am so glad to have been of service. I came myself with my driver to make sure that you could be on your way to Kampala speedily. The rain has stopped so it should be a good journey from now on."

He waved, turned and went back to the lorry.

One twenty a.m. The Land Rover stopped at the steps leading up to Nakasero Hospital in Kampala. The consultant saw Mike Barker at two a.m. His examination was brief and then he turned to Boyd and said, "There's nothing we can do now, Hamish. He's dead. Can't really say when. Sad, really. Good man. Very fit. Fastest thing on two legs I've seen."

39

Elaine Barker came into the room and stood in the shadows just behind the medical men. Her arms still reached round, clutching herself. She moved forwards and tugged the sleeve of the consultant's shirt.

"Mike will be well enough to travel, won't he? We go on long leave next month."

Jane Cartwright could feel the tear as it glistened on her cheek. She turned and left the room. It was only minutes after she had found a bench in the corridor that she was joined by Hamish Boyd. The Medical Officer sat beside her, took her hand and said, "Tell me, Jane…"

He coughed and then it took him time to say, "When are you due?"

No more would she face the Mountains of the Moon.

THE BRICK OUTHOUSE

I was about to leave a department store in North London when I saw a young woman with some very large bags struggling to leave through the rotating doorway. Her difficulties did not mask her elegance and it set me wondering – what did she do… what might she do… for a living?

I'm strolling among the counters in this, the finest store in London outside the West End. What am I looking for? Clothes? No, I am well stocked with things to wear. Shoes, then? I bought a pair only last week. Male grooming smellies? Now that's a thought. But I had come in for more than that. Much more. Inspiration, stimulation, encouragement and not least of all motivation, these are my current necessities, not toiletries. The creative talent needs topping up now and again when the well has run dry. Only temporarily, of course. You can't buy that off the shelf, can you, however prestigious the store. But your surroundings do help, as everyone knows. Where was Rossellini when he first set eyes on Bergmann, Howard Hawks – or was it Howard Hughes – when he gained his first glimpse of Marilyn Munroe?

The muse has eluded me all through the store from Second Floor lingerie, to Ground Floor cosmetics, and down to kitchen wear in the Basement, and here I am near the door and the only way now is out.

I catch sight of her as she passes through the revolving door ahead of me. I watch her through the several panes of glass. She isn't Hollywood beautiful, but she has that something about her that demands a long look. A model she isn't, that is certain, not the unnatural walk and sullen pouting features of the professional clothes hangers. More Pinewood or Ealing Studios. But with all my experience, I can assure anyone that she does have star quality.

She has struggled out of the door with the bulky carrier bags emblazoned with the Store's logo. A closer inspection is needed.

The turning door spews me forward and I am on the pavement in time to see her forty yards or so to my right, moving easily with a feline grace. Her camel-hair coat, unbelted and capacious, is a little on the heavy side for so fine a day, but what matter. She flicks a glance over her shoulder as she strolls on. So appealing. And now she's stopping at a pavement café. She lowers the bags as she moves to an empty chair. What movement, what stylishness, what class. This is exactly what I have been looking for. For my latest movie, of course, but I mustn't rush things. One has to be sure, there's too much at stake. And – come to think of it – a long black coffee, an Americano, would not come amiss at this time. The table here is far enough away from her to be able to observe without being obvious.

She is ordering, turning her head up and tilting it back to engage the waiter and in the movement, exposing an expanse of creamy white throat. I can see it. I can see the scene here and now. I will re-write it just for her. No, I will write a whole new act. It's no use playing at it. It's strange, isn't it, what seals one's decisions? That one fleeting movement did it. I make a frame with my hands and hold them up to view her through the oblong shape. That's it.

That is definitely it.

While she is waiting for her coffee – what will it be, latte, cappuccino, definitely not skinnychino like they call it in Australia? Now she is on her mobile. That look, that wistful smile. It has to be a lover.

*

"Yea, Vladimir, I'm at the usual place. Don't come yet, there's a funny geezer here. He followed me out of the store. Now he's sitting five tables away. He's just been looking through his hands at me. Yes, it was like he was holding a camera, but I didn't see one… Is he a store detective? Could be, I suppose, but he's so obvious… Well, he's wearing this old-fashioned suit and a paisley silk waistcoat. And he's got a black hat like the godfathers used to wear in the old movies. Stands out like a sore thumb. Was the trip worthwhile? I should coco. Four of those dresses you wanted, top of the range, and the bits and pieces of underwear. You can tick 'em off your list. But what do I do about this creep?… What's that? Stay put and see what happens, you say. OK but I don't like it. I've got form, you know. It's my neck not yours. He's still eyeing me as though he doesn't want me to know he's doing it… I know, I know, even if I'm caught, it'll only be a ticking off, but we lose the gear and that took a lot of trouble."

*

What next? Go over, sit down alongside her and say, "You're just what I'm looking for, for my latest film, 'Wait Until the Moon Comes Up'. I can make a star out of you." Mm… Though it's true, it sounds a little too like a corny chat up line. Maybe I should just scribble her a note and

43

drop it on the table in front of her with my visiting card, 'Ring this number to hear something to your advantage'. No, that won't do either. Too much like those little square notices they stick on lamp-posts saying, 'If you want high earnings and have got a car, phone this number'. I've got to do something soon; you don't come across one like this every day.

*

"Come on, Vladimir. Give me something. He's still sitting there. I know he isn't going to move until I do… What?… Get up casual like and go round the back of Marks and Sparks and you'll sort him out there. OK but keep me out of the rough stuff. You know I don't like it."

*

I knew as much, she's on the move, gathering up all those bags. Money on the table. Damn. Please, please, please, don't let my chance slip away just like that. Wait a bit, though. I can hardly pursue her down the street, can I? She'll think I'm a stalker or whatever they call people like that and that's definitely not my style. There's always a silver lining though. You lose some and then you win some. It'll give me time for the Formula One drive I've been promising myself. On with the fireproof suit and helmet and sit with my nerves all-a-jangle at the start line at Silverstone. It's the sort of test I need this afternoon. Well, it won't actually be Silverstone; no, certainly not. I'll have you know, X-Box really isn't a pathetic substitute.

*

"All clear, Vladimir. He's up and gone the other way. I can see him properly now that he's stood up. I think it's all for the best, really. You should see the shoulders on him. What?... Yeah, don't get the hump with me. I know you are. But not this one. He's built like the proverbial... What do you think I mean? The proverbial brick outhouse, that's what I mean. You and your English. I'm on my way."

OBULANI

'Ex Africa semper aliquid novi' (*out of Africa always something new*), said *Pliny the Elder. How true! This story was born out of several strange experiences when I worked in Uganda, though I have to declare none was quite as strange as this story.*

"Come in. I've got a job for you."

Superintendent Mellor indicated the chair and I sat down. I was a young police inspector and had arrived a week earlier in Tororo, a Uganda town close to the border with Kenya.

"We've just had a message from Mulabi village. There's been a robbery there. A gang of Africans attacked an Indian shop. Fortunately, they didn't kill anyone, but they sound like the lot who have been in the area for the last couple of months. They will have moved on by now, but I want you to go down there and see what you can find out."

"How far is Mulabi?"

"It's about 35 miles from here, only a tiny place, a mile off the Busia road. The robbery happened in the early hours of this morning. The shop keeper, Muljibhai Patel, had his car stolen by the thieves so he couldn't come here himself. They don't have a telephone there and the driver of a local cotton lorry brought the report. Your Swahili is a bit thin, so you'll need to take one of the detectives with you. I don't know who is available – they're a busy lot. When they are free they tend to wait under the mango tree in the compound."

I nodded my understanding to the Superintendent and he continued, "I don't suppose you will have handled anything like this before, but I thought it will be good experience for you."

It was now 10.00 a.m. on the 5th October 1952. I had only been in the country for three months – all that time in Kampala doing what they called Familiarity Training and basic Swahili – and was feeling as green as a whole meadow of grass. There were no detectives in the charge office but the corporal on duty said there might be one outside. Failing that, they would all be out on enquiries.

As I went out to the compound and stood near my parked van I heard someone calling, "Sir... sir!"

The voice came from near the mango tree in the corner of the compound, where an African was squatting on his haunches in the shade. He was dressed in dark trousers and a white shirt and his face sported long sideburns and a bushy moustache.

"Sir, you are going to Mulabi to investigate the robbery. I am your detective."

Thankfully his English was good. My Swahili was only sufficient for a few greetings and I would not have got far on this enquiry with that. He looked promising and, before anyone else could claim him, I told him to get into the van.

"And you are... ?"

"I am detective Sitanyule."

We followed the Busia road. Red dust followed us in clouds so I kept the van's windows closed. It wasn't long before the cab of the van felt cool, in fact downright chilly. I was puzzled by this, because the temperature outside was in the 80s. I put it out of my mind. I had enough to think about.

To make conversation I asked, "Do you know Mulabi?"

"Yes, I know Mulabi. It is not a big village, one street only and Pateli's is the only shop."

The rest of the conversation until we reached Mulabi was limited to his giving me directions.

When we arrived, I could see that the heavy wooden door of the shop hung crazily on its broken hinges, testimony to how the robbers had made their entry. Muljibhai Patel half sat, half lay on a wooden steamer chair on the veranda near the door, taking sips from a cup of water. His head was heavily bandaged with cloth torn from a shirt. Neither he nor any of his family spoke English well enough for me to be of any use in making the necessary enquiries and so the detective took over using Swahili.

After two hours of inspecting the shop and the area, asking questions and writing statements, we seemed to have done all that was necessary.

We were ready to depart when the detective said, "There is one more thing," and he returned to the shop, went inside, and walked around sniffing.

"It's what I thought. Lugbara."

"What do you mean, 'Lugbara'?"

"The robbers were of the Lugbara tribe. They are not local men. They are from the West Nile district."

"And how do you know that?"

"Using my nose told me."

I decided not to pursue this any further. So he used his

nose. I was new to the country. Maybe this is what detectives did here.

We drove back to Tororo. It was early evening and the Superintendent had gone. As I parked in the police station compound, the detective said, "There are only a few Lugbara living around here and they are all in Nyangole village. We will go there tonight and find them. I will be here at ten o' clock. If we are earlier we shall not surprise them."

Seeing this as a chance for success in my first case at Tororo, I nodded my agreement.

I drove into the compound at ten. The lights of my van swung round the area, but I could see no-one waiting. I parked and switched off the lights and no sooner had I done this than the detective appeared.

"I am ready," he said, opening the passenger door and climbing in. He told me the route to take and we drove in silence.

"Stop here. The car will be safe."

In this part of the world, a village is not as we know it. It is a network of paths with huts dotted here and there separated by small plots of cultivated land. To European eyes, there is no structure and no focal point. I was totally dependent on the detective now. We walked along narrow rutted paths and in the dark I stumbled frequently, barely resisting the urge to curse out loud. It was difficult keeping up with him, but dark as it was, I could still see his form hurrying ahead of me.

He stopped in a small clearing and I could just make

out that he was pointing to a hut.

"Here," he whispered. "This is where we will find the Lugbara."

I suddenly felt scared. Just the two of us, but it was too late to do anything about this. I had a torch in my hand, but so far had not used it, for fear of being spotted. The detective put his shoulder to the door and heaved. With no noise, it caved in.

I followed him into the hut, stooping low to avoid the thatching of the roof, and switched on my torch. In its beam, I could see figures stirring on the floor under their blankets. One of them half sat up. With incredible speed the detective swung forward as through making a ferocious backhand stroke in tennis. But this was no game. I saw the panga – the machete to be found everywhere in Africa – flash in his hand. I'll never know where it came from, though I'm sure he didn't have it when we entered the hut. The slashing blow removed the man's head cleanly. Simultaneously, there was the sound of a shot magnified into an explosion by the closeness of the walls. The blood was spurting from the headless neck, but the man must have fired the revolver at the same moment as the panga hit him.

"Take the pistol, sir. It is important evidence."

I leant forward and took the gun away from the man's hand, wrapping it in the blanket. As I did so, the other people who had been in the hut on our arrival bolted and scrambled through the door. I had no idea how many there were since I hadn't counted them when we entered. I turned to look for the detective, but he wasn't there. I shone my torch around outside and called out for detective Sitanyule but there was no response.

I don't know how long I spent looking around but there was still no sign of anyone and I made my way – with great difficulty, I must say – to where I thought I had left the van. At last I found it. There was no one there and I was panicking. Where the hell had the detective gone? How I had relied on him. The whole venture was a ghastly mess and outside my control. There was only one thing to do. Get to the superintendent as quickly as I could.

I drove to his house and hammered on the door. After a few minutes he appeared, rubbing his eyes.

"Do you know what hour it is? It's two o'clock in the morning."

Despite the rough greeting, he sat me down and listened to my account, saying nothing but nodding from time to time.

"You can't do anything more now. Go home and get to bed. I'll take it from here. You come and see me first thing in the morning."

I reported to Mellor at eight. He had the pistol lying on the blanket on his desk in front of us, a Webley .45 calibre.

"I find your account of what happened astonishing and I'll come back to that, but first I'll fill you in about the rest of the night. I went to the place you described, and the body was there. It's in the mortuary now. Everyone from the hut had fled and our men are out trying to round them up. We found Muljibhai's car at the back of the hut covered over with banana fronds."

All of this was reassuring. I was beginning to feel less

apprehensive, but why then did I feel so uneasy at his next question?

"Did you get the detective's name?"

"Yes, sir, He said it was Sitanyule."

"I've something to tell you. You're not long in Africa so you may find it hard to believe."

The superintendent was an 'Old Africa Hand', with a reputation for knowing as much as anyone about folk lore and he also spoke several local languages – it was common knowledge that he had his own sleeping dictionary – so I found myself holding my breath waiting for him to continue.

"Your description is a perfect fit for Sergeant Obulani. **Sitanyule Obulani.** A damn good man, the finest detective I have ever had."

I let out my breath.

"Well that's a relief to know who he is," but I wondered why Mellor's gaze had had gone down, boring holes in the desk top.

I waited. "Sir…?"

"He's dead."

I started shaking; what else had gone wrong?

"But he was alive enough last night when he disappeared. What happened?"

My stomach turned over, all kinds of thoughts racing through my mind.

"Was there anything I could have done?"

"No, no. You don't understand. Why should you? You've only been here just over the week. He was killed two months ago. By a gang of robbers."

I tried to speak and was tongue-tied.

Mellor continued as if I wasn't present.

"You see, he was shot with a .45 pistol. His assassin escaped but was identified as being a Lugbara."

There was nothing I could say. I was out of my depth. Totally.

The superintendent fidgeted with the edge of the blanket on which the pistol lay, obviously grappling with some unresolved problem. Then he said, "An incident of this kind is so serious it must be reported in detail to the Commissioner."

I waited for him to continue. He didn't.

"Sir?"

He looked up, smiled wryly and said, "You see my dilemma, don't you, Peter? Not to put too fine a point on it… our Commissioner… is a little short on imagination.

GREMLINS ON THE LINE

I came across the word 'Gremlins' recently. What follows is the memory it jogged.

From the late 1800s until the 1960s, the railways of East Africa (Kenya, Tanganyika and Uganda) were run by an organisation later to be known as East African Railways and Harbours. It was a well-run authority with a good safety record, when the wide range of hazards is considered. This account is about the interesting – bizarre even – finding of an enquiry into a serious accident.

The main line from Mombasa on the Kenyan coast to Kampala in Uganda is about a eight hundred and fifty miles long. It starts by passing through plains, often subject to flooding, but in the railway's earliest days these plains were notorious for the man-eating lions, whose predatory activities halted the construction of the track for months at a time. They even took one of the big game hunters sent to clear them. An exciting account of this is given in the book 'The Man Eaters of Tsavo' by John Patterson (first published in 1907!).

From the plains, the railway rises from near sea level to over six thousand feet at Nairobi. From then on, remarkable engineering, with what may seem to us today as very primitive equipment, completed its descent many hundreds of feet down into the great Rift Valley. Having crossed the valley, it then had to go up and out of it reaching the highest point of any railway in the

Commonwealth. Once in Uganda, its passage over the vast Mpologoma swamp had to be negotiated and then on to bridging the mighty Nile river, where it pours out of Lake Victoria.

The scale of hazards is not hard to imagine. They went far beyond the physical features. For instance, outside the stations, the line was single track and in the early days a system known as 'paper line clear' was in use to avoid one train leaving a station meeting another one coming from the opposite direction. This was one obvious source of danger and, after one dreadful head-on smash, the method being used was overhauled throughout the whole system and all sections of the line – particularly branch lines – were made subject to a mechanical system which was virtually accident proof.

Of course, there were many other hazards. Washaways due to heavy rain and flooding, obstacles such as boulders, and large animals using the permanent way as a track were some of these. Another was the removal of 'steel keys'. These keys were six-inch-long metal wedges which held the rails firmly into the notches of the steel sleepers. Take away a number of these from a section of rail and the consequent looseness of the rail could cause a derailment. It didn't help that these steel keys were perfect source material for local blacksmiths making spear heads. The Permanent Way Inspection Department made regular and thorough tours of the track to check for hazards of any kind.

The Motive Power Department was responsible, not only for the mechanical condition of the locomotives and all other rolling stock, but also for the testing of drivers to ensure their capability for the nature of locomotive being driven.

The Engineering Department looked after signals and all other mechanical aspects of running the Railway. The Traffic Department was responsible for all facets of the carriage of goods and an important part of this was to ensure that loads in wagons were well-balanced. This was particularly important in the case of the American Covered Bogies (beloved of the hoboes in the USA and regularly featuring in films). These had to be very carefully loaded and marshalled on the train since they were more likely to jump off the track than any other wagons.

In the 1940s there was a fatal railway accident in Kenya. It caused considerable damage to the permanent way and to the locomotive and rolling stock. With an accident of this nature, it was customary for an enquiry to be held by a magistrate. Representatives of each of the departments mentioned earlier were called to give evidence.

The District Motive Power Superintendent, the Locomotive Foreman from the nearest workshops, and the driver and fireman testified. From their evidence it was concluded that all the mechanical and safety features of the locomotive were in order. The driver and fireman were fully trained and competent, were physically fit and sober and had met all the operating requirements. There was nothing about the department's operations that could have contributed to the accident.

And so it went on, with responsible officers from each of the departments declaring that they could find nothing from their areas of accountability that would have caused the crash. All these officers who gave evidence were recalled and interrogated again and still they affirmed the competence in the way their departments had operated.

At last the magistrate called all the parties together. He declared that three days of enquiry had given him no information that could show how the accident had happened. He consequently could only find the accident was due to the activities of gremlins on the line. So had he recorded his verdict!

The term 'gremlin' was Royal Air Force slang. It was originally applied to a mischievous mythical being that sabotaged aircraft, although later it was applied to any other inexplicable mechanical failings. It was first used in the 1920s by the British pilots stationed in Malta, the Middle East, and India. Much later, of course, the name was adopted by a film, 'Gremlins', which revived the mischievous being idea.

JUST A FAIRY TALE REALLY

I watched a friend who ran a conference centre in a listed building grapple with the conflicting instructions of the Local Authority and another Authority for structural changes to the building for emergency exits. His frustration – and threat to income – when public bodies made totally different demands was unlike anything I had ever experienced. He shook his head and said, "It's like a fairy tale."

"Help me. Please help me"

She had heard the thump from where she stood by the open back door of her public house, taking the cool night air before turning in. By the light of her torch, she could see him lying there, on his back, moaning lowly. He must have fallen from the top of the wall. She knew the stout little figure by sight, even though he was in the unusual position of being stretched out flat on his back, an ugly looking jemmy lying near his right hand. Without any doubt he was badly hurt.

With her mobile she rang the emergency number and after that she could only try to comfort him while she waited, holding his hand and wiping the moisture from his wide forehead. He must have fallen from the top of the wall and at this time of night he could have only been there for the wrong reasons. The wall was well over six feet high and he was such a short, rotund man to get up there. She took off her jacket and rolled it up and eased it under his head.

He groaned again and the words, "Thank you. You are

so kind," tiptoed from his mouth.

The reassuring sound of the ambulance's siren broke the quiet of the night. The paramedics were brisk and businesslike, oozing capability.

"You've done well, but it would have been better if you hadn't put that coat under his head. Still you weren't to know, were you?"

Once the patient was aboard the ambulance, a paramedic turned to the woman.

"Was it you who phoned for us?"

She nodded.

"Can I have your name please for the record? Mrs. Alison Kinsmen? Thank you love," and with that they were off, siren blaring and blue lamp strobing away.

She didn't mind him calling her love, a sort of old-fashioned touch from a kind man, wasn't it?

The injured man knew nothing of his arrival at the hospital but now here he was lying on the trolley in a corridor. How long he had been there he didn't know. There was no clock and no one to talk to. Not that he wanted to talk. It was daylight and he felt, rather than saw, people moving around. A voice cut into his personal mist and a shape bent over him.

"Hello, squire, I'm from Huckster and Huckster, the law firm who can get you a good deal. You've probably seen our adverts. They tell me you've had an accident. But we all know there's no such thing as an accident is there? Someone's always to blame and that's where we come in. Now, down to business. You've had a nasty experience and someone has to pay for it. Don't you agree, squire?"

There was no reply. No movement.

"I can take that as a 'yes', then?… And another thing, this hanging around in corridors doesn't do much for the nerves, does it? We can get you something for that, too. Here's my card – office and mobile numbers on there. Give me a ring when you feel like it and I'll be in toot sweet. You've got a pretty good case, squire, if you ask me."

He waved a small card near the patient's head.

"Get in touch any time, as soon as you're a bit better."

The patient made no move to take the card and so the lawyers' representative tucked it under the pillow. He read the name off the clipboard at the end of the trolley, entered it into a little notebook and walked off, fishing in his pocket for a cigarette as he went.

It was lunch time in the Royal Coach and Horses public house. Alison Kinsmen was short-staffed and she was taking her turn at pulling pints. Now the rush had slowed to a trickle and she found herself thinking about the man who had fallen from her wall two nights ago. A deep-throated cough ended her daydream.

"What can I get you, sir?"

She looked up to see a long cadaverous face and a dark blue suit with a spotted bow tie.

"Mrs Alison Kinsmen?"

"Yes."

She looked expectantly at him.

"I'm from the District Council. We have been taking a look at the wall at the back of your property and we have found that it contravenes regulations."

"It's been there three hundred years and no one has said anything about it in all that time. My father was landlord before me, and his father before him."

"This is no time for sentimentality, Mrs Kinsmen. I am talking of today. It is too high. Too high by 8cm, to be precise. We shall recommend that you take it all down and rebuild it."

"But it's as sturdy as ever. I've just had it re-pointed."

"That's not the point."

He certainly hadn't spotted the pun.

"After all, our risk analysis shows the act of removing a bit off the top is bound to weaken it lower down and we can't risk that can we? We shall be serving you with an official notice. Good day to you."

And that happened on the Monday. On Wednesday afternoon as she was about to put the cloth over the pumps a plump, jolly looking man entered the inn.

"Sorry, I'm just shutting up. I'll be opening again at six."

"I haven't come for sustenance, dear lady. Oh no, I'm on business. I'm from the County Council. I really must ask you to give me a few minutes of your valuable leisure time. May we sit?"

The man took off his straw hat and planted his body firmly at a table near the bar.

"On second thoughts, it would be a shame not to sample such a renowned ale – The Royal Coach is known for it throughout the county, you know."

Alison Kinsmen took the teacloth from the triple X pump, worked a pint into a glass and brought it round to the man. She stood over him, hands on hips, her stance for the drunks who didn't know when to leave.

"Now what's it all about this time? My wall again, I suppose?"

"Well, yes, it is. By the way, this ale is really excellent."

"Go on, tell me the worst. How long do I have before I have to take it down?"

"Well, no. Most certainly, no. You mustn't do anything to that wall. And to take it down, to alter it in any shape or form will cause you all sorts of problems."

"I must say that's a relief. Why the change of heart? Only two days ago your man said I would be served with a notice."

"Not our man, dear lady. He's from an entirely different authority. They probably will still serve the notice, but I have to tell you that your admirable public house is now within the extended Conservation Area and it has been declared a Grade Two listed building. You can't make any external alterations and that includes knocking down or otherwise altering the wall. It's over three hundred years old, you know."

"Let's get this straight. That lot tell me the wall has to come down and you lot tell me I can't do anything with it. Go away, will you, and get your act together."

"Oh, I do wish it were that simple. The fact is, both our departments are legally correct and I'm afraid it's a dilemma you will have to solve yourself. There's nothing I can do."

He wiped the beer froth from his mouth, put his straw hat on his head and, with a "Very good day to you, madam," departed. Alison Kinsmen was so annoyed she only realised when it was too late that he had not paid for the beer.

On Friday morning, before opening time, as she left by the back door to go shopping, a car drove into the parking space. A long, lean man pulled himself out of it and called to her.

"Mrs. Kinsmen? Glad I've caught you before you left. I'm Witherspoon from the Safety Observance Authority. I'd like a word, please."

And soon this one word had spun itself into scores, hundreds even. The upshot was that Mr Witherspoon left half an hour later, having informed Alison Kinsmen that she had not taken all due and reasonable care to make her wall safe – no non-slip coating on its top for example – thereby occasioning the accident.

"Serious consideration is being given to your prosecution," was his Parthian shot.

All of this was now too much for the good landlady. She could no longer bear the thought of shopping, so she turned on her heel, went back inside and pulled herself a pint. When she opened, a short man with wandering eyes was her first customer. He took his drink to a far table and was engrossed in reading the local newspaper. Suddenly he burst into a spontaneous rant.

To the world at large he declared, "Would you flipping believe it?" He read aloud from the paper. "The Town Says Goodbye to Mystery Man. After a serious fall last Saturday night, a man was taken to the General Hospital where he died yesterday. To most he was simply 'Aitch'. His full name was a mystery. As far as we can ascertain, he leaves no relatives. He kept himself to himself, was always cheerful and had an old-fashioned courtesy. The funeral will be held next Friday.

"Well, would you credit it? He's gone and died on me and just as I was setting up a nice little action for his injuries. Not even any relatives to pursue."

The lawyer's representative lifted his head from the paper.

"Sorry, Mrs K, I didn't see you there... Here, every cloud has one, hasn't it? A little bird told me you've got big problems. How about us looking after them for you? One of our senior partners is an MP, got a bit of clout in the right quarters, if you get my drift, love."

Love from this man, she did not like.

It is three months now since Alison Kinsmen left the Royal Coach and Horses. She had been declared officially bankrupt. The white van in the car park is packed with builders' equipment and two young men are carrying long silver metal poles from the vehicle towards the hostelry.

"What's them for, then?" asks a curious passer-by.

"They're going to liven the old place up. These are for a bit of artistic dancing, know what I mean."

He winks, taps the side of his nose, and he and his mate continue to carry their load in through the back door.

COME HOME TO ROOST

Someone I know – a man of 50+, had worked for the same company ever since leaving school. It was taken over by an asset stripper. I found the ruthlessness they showed in their methods of coercing key staff not to leave beyond my belief. In my book, it was immoral. It left me feeling they needed some strong 'comeuppance' – say, as in this story.

Two am. The ringing of the phone nudged me from the deep sleep of the small hours. Since retiring, I didn't get the night calls that I used to get when I was in the Police Service.

I answered it. "Bob Ball. Who is it?"

"Mike."

The voice sounded subdued. I couldn't think of any Mikes.

Tentatively I tried, "Mike Lingard?"

"Yes.

I was about to say, "What do you want at this time of night?" but the tone of his voice said something gentler was required.

"Mike. Good to hear you. Long time."

'I had to talk to someone."

The words were slurred.

"Mike, what is it?"

"I can't go on like this. It's become too much. The bastards are going to screw me."

There was a pause and I thought he had left the phone.

Then his voice whispered in my ear, "I think I'll end it all."

"Take it easy, Mike. Do you want to talk about it?"

I couldn't make out the response.

"Mike, are you still there?"

I heard a sound.

"Are you at home?"

I thought I heard the word 'Yes'.

"You'd better not drive. I'll come over to you."

As I drove, I thought about Mike. We had met several years earlier, got on well, and had taken to meeting for a meal out every six weeks. I was a widower and he was separated from his wife and children. Before I retired, I had been an Inspector in CID, but I now did part-time work as an insurance investigator. He had worked for the same company for twenty-five years, ever since leaving school. The last time we met, he had been unusually agitated. There had been a management buy-out, a venture capital company had taken over and he was miserable with the way they were being managed.

"They couldn't care less about us, they're just setting us up to strip the assets out," he said. "I know I'm not the top brass, but I don't expect to be treated like a lump of muck. I've got to get out."

"If that's the way you feel, it would be the best thing," I had offered, and from then until now, I had thought no more of it.

I rang the doorbell. The door inched open and a face peered out, bleary eyed.

"You'd better come in," was all he said, and without

waiting for me, he made his way into the lounge. There was a whisky bottle with an inch left in it on the coffee table.

"Something's really got to you, Mike. Care to tell me about it?"

He sat looking at me for minutes, as if composing a statement in his mind.

"They've got me over a barrel, Bob."

"What do you mean?"

"You know I said I couldn't stomach any more of the lot who took our company over? Well, it must have shown."

I smiled, "I reckon it did, just a bit."

"A director cornered me and said if I was thinking of leaving, I'd better think again. If I left, they'd slap an injunction on me to stop me going to any other company that was a competitor. For a year. Well, we're not in a very big industry, so every other company in the industry is a competitor and I would be unemployable for the first year and then very likely for ever."

"If that wasn't in your contract, they couldn't do that."

"Ah, but you don't know the cunning bastards. The director reminded me that I had bought some shares in the company three years ago when they took us over. I was told at the time it was a good thing; to show that we had faith in the company. I bought a thousand pounds worth and I could hardly afford that – some of the senior people bought large amounts… "

I interrupted him, "I don't see what this has got to do with their stopping you working for anyone else."

"Just hear me out."

At least he was talking now.

"With the issue of the shares came thirty pages of bumf, most of it in legalese. You wouldn't suspect anything underhand with a simple thing like buying a few shares in your company would you? So I just signed the wad of paper they pushed in front of me and got on with my job. Anyhow, buried in these papers was a clause which said by signing, I was subject to certain restrictions and one of these was that if I left the company I couldn't work for a competitor for a year."

"But you could work in another line for that time."

He had perked up while he was talking, but my question touched a nerve. He spat the next words as though firing a gun.

"You weren't listening. After all my time in this industry and at my age what else do I know? What else could I do apart from pumping petrol or sitting at a supermarket check out? In my book that makes me unemployable. I wouldn't earn enough to hold things together for my kids."

"OK, Mike. I understand... "

"Yeah. I bet you don't. Here's the punch line. I got a letter from the company's lawyers today, some fancy firm with an address in the City of London."

He held a letter up and read from it. "*...If you as an employee will not honour a legal agreement the company will not hesitate to take action in the High Court. If this is found to be necessary, we shall ask for costs against you and these are bound to be high.* They're going to hang me out on the washing line."

"They're just trying to put the frighteners on.

Whatever the letter says a court wouldn't uphold this."

"Well they're damn well succeeding. I'm as frightened as hell. I can't risk going to court. It's not as though there is any real justice in this country now. Maybe I would win but it'll cost a bomb for lawyers and I'll be bankrupt, no credit and no hope. My wife can look after herself, but what about the boys?"

"I'll do some checking with a lawyer I know."

"How soon can you do that?"

"It'll depend on when I can get hold of the guy, but I'll be as fast as I can."

My becoming involved seemed to have settled him.

"I've got to go. Will you be alright now?"

He nodded, and I let myself out.

It was now 5.00 am. I managed a little sleep, but I was haunted by visions of Mike's frightened face. At 9.00 am, I was lucky with the lawyer. He was in his office and happy to talk.

He supported my view but he went on, "That's off the record, old boy. I can't give a proper opinion without going into the detail."

I could see the pound signs whirling round, like a petrol pump filling a three litre 4x4. I didn't know how Mike would react to this information. It wasn't what he would want to hear, but I felt duty bound to call him. There was no reply. I left a message on his answer machine to ring me.

Two days went by and he hadn't rung back. It worried me, since I could still see his tortured face. I kept trying for another couple of days and then I gave it up. By now, there were enough messages on his machine.

And then there was a phone call. But it wasn't Mike. It was an insurance company, wanting me to look into a fire that had taken place the previous night at a warehouse. Heartlands Building Supplies. I phoned around; the people from the police and the fire service I needed to talk to were at the scene. I drove straight there, arriving about eleven. It was a steaming, stinking, smoking mess. The warehouse buildings were gutted, black and smouldering. The offices had no windows and the smoke had streaked all the brickwork with black. Heaven knows what had happened to all the office equipment. It was in an area where what hadn't been burnt would have been looted by now.

To my question, the fire chief said, "Too early to be absolutely certain but arson's the hot favourite."

I'm not sure he meant the pun.

"It burned slowly in one of the stacks of block board, building up intense heat, and then the lot went up."

"What about the fire alarm?"

"That's a mystery. It looks as though it wasn't working."

I turned to the uniform police sergeant who was standing listening to the conversation.

"Have you found out anything about that?"

"No. There's no one here who can give any answers."

At that moment, a large, glossy BMW drove in through the site gates. I walked over with the sergeant to where a red-faced man was easing himself from the driver's seat. He stood peering at the chaos in front of him, shaking his head, and then he turned towards us.

"Fordyce. I'm the managing director of Midas Holdings for this region."

We must have both looked blank.

He spoke again, tetchily, louder, "Midas Holdings – we own Heartlands Building Supplies – and this was our regional head office. There was over a million pounds worth of stock. How did it happen?"

"We were hoping you could shed some light on this. Who was responsible for the alarm system? The fire people say it wasn't working."

I could already see a get-out for the insurance company.

"It's down to Lingard. He's the manager of the depot."

Lingard. Could it be Mike? Of course. He always spoke of HBS – not Heartlands Building Supplies.

"Can I talk to him?"

"If you can find him. He's been off sick and he hasn't been answering his phone."

Fordyce was walking to where the fire chief was directing his men.

I felt the vibration of my mobile and answered it. It was the insurance company calling me.

"You'll love this," said Mandy, my contact in the company. "Are you ready for it? HBS are no longer insured with us."

There was triumph in her voice.

"What? I understood they were a long-standing client."

"They were, but Mr. Lingard, rang us two weeks ago when he got the renewal notice and said he was being pushed on budgets and had to shop around. He faxed last

Friday to say they weren't renewing. This morning a Mr. Fordyce rang my manager who thought they were still with us, that's why he called you out." Sigh. "It *would* help if people went through the proper channels."

"That's the story of life, Mandy."

I rang off. Fordyce could stew for a bit. Hearing Mike's name had made me curious, so I decided to stay for a while. I saw the sergeant walking towards the site gate with that look on his face that only policemen have when they unearth a gem.

"The security company's CCTV picked up a man going in through HBS's front door at eleven twenty-eight last night. Two of the staff identified him as Lingard. Positive, no doubts whatsoever. So that's it, then. We've cracked it."

I suppose I wasn't surprised, really. In the state he'd been in, it was not surprising that Mike had taken his revenge on the company and damn the consequences.

That evening I was home, tidying up some correspondence. I fell to thinking about how we never know about people, when the phone rang.

"Sergeant Williams. We met at the warehouse fire. I thought you'd be interested in this. I believe you know Lingard?"

"Yes, I know Mike. Known him for years."

I wondered what was coming next.

"Have you found him?"

"In a manner of speaking."

"What's that mean?"

"He was admitted to the General Hospital at six

yesterday evening; having downed lord knows how many painkillers and the best part of a bottle of Scotch. Last night he was on the operating table. Never came round from the time he was brought in. They say he died at eleven thirty... Well, aren't you going to say something?"

BEACH LANDING

On Phillip Island, just off the Mornington Peninsular in the State of Victoria in Australia, a remarkable event takes place each night.

Gradually they had amassed over the past two hours. Their transport was parked well out of sight of the beaches. Now, as they grouped around the assembly points, drinking coffee or just talking, there was an air of expectation. Anticipation. The sound of a host of different tongues blended to an unintelligible, but not unpleasant swell, like the movement of the sea that was so close. United nations, but not UN. There was a clear-cut aim that brought such a multi-national body together.

Now came the time for the briefings. There was a shifting from one foot to another, uncertain of what would come next. Eventually all had closed up to the nearest marshal. Now the quality of the training was apparent. The marshals were well informed and in control. They may not have been able to converse in all the languages, but they communicated.

Black bags were issued for personal items that were prohibited from the action areas. The parties moved off in single file following the guide lights along the prepared tracks to the concrete emplacements with an unimpaired view of the beaches. Nearly two hours gone, and everyone was in place.

"Where will they land?"

"Will they rush the beach or use stealth?"

"Shall I be able to say I was there and part of it all?"

The waiting and uncertainty was beginning to tell. An arm goes out to point at a swimmer. No, it was imagination, kelp swirling in the tide. And so it goes on, an arm pointing over there, muffled voices rising and falling like the sea. Night glasses trained on the surf, the viewer impatient to see action.

Is there a sense of growing disappointment? Maybe they are not coming tonight and then we will have to muster again.

And then they came. At first one, picking his way through rocks to find the largest shield. Then came more to join the vanguard. A dozen this time, safety in numbers. They crossed the open beach and disappeared into the dunes, outflanking the emplacements and the multi-national force that occupied them. Muted words rippled around.

"Was that the lot? There didn't seem to be many. What shall we do now?"

"Stay firm. There will be more. You will see as much action as you can take soon."

Another dozen or so hurried ashore and then more repeated the movements, all disappearing into the dunes. They moved as though, in their turn, they were as well trained as those marshalling the force. Thoroughly conditioned for what lay ahead of them.

So, who were the invaders? Hostile troops? No. Aliens? Don't believe in them! Beasts from the deep, then? Well yes, but not the kind to be found in horror fiction. In fact they were penguins; fairy penguins.

This is Phillip Island, Victoria, Australia. To this beach,

each evening throughout the year, hundreds of fairy penguins return from their fishing many kilometers off shore. In summer time, between a thousand and fifteen hundred leave their nesting grounds in the dunes every night, stay three or four days at sea and then come back. The marvel is that this happens daily, on a rota basis, as it were. And it is always the same small section of the Victorian coast.

Once the penguins have crossed the beach, the best place to see them is from the concrete seating and then the complex of boardwalks that the Phillip Island Nature Park has built through the sand dunes alongside the well-trodden paths that the penguins follow. The lighting provided enables the visitor to watch them comfortably and without disturbing them, as they trek up the inclines, following the grooves in the sand dunes that have been trodden smooth by thousands of pairs of webbed feet.

It is hard to resist the temptation to attribute human characteristics and thoughts to these diminutive creatures. Here comes a group now, plodding their way up, their wings held out to provide balance. And then one stops, and it is as though he is wiping his brow with his wing.

"Can't take a step farther."

The two penguins immediately behind walk straight into him.

"Silly place to stop. Get a move on. We haven't got all night, you know."

But having better sense than humans, there is no road rage, no mindless gestures.

Another goes flop on his belly.

"That's it. I'm all in. I'm staying here until morning."

Tail end Charlene of the next group stops and turns off onto a small side track.

"It's been some night, girls. I'm home, don't know about you. Watch out for me when you come back down. See you later."

And off she goes.

The two thousand or so watchers have witnessed the incredible spectacle of the beach landing and the yomp over the dunes by the fairy penguins. Now the watchers drift off to their transport – coaches back to Melbourne or their own cars.

One last warning, though, booms through the public-address system.

"Before you drive off, look under your cars. You don't want to squash a penguin, do you?"

IN ISOLATION

It is easy to forget how far medical practices have come in our lifetime. The older one gets the more remarkable it feels. When in Britain did we last experience an epidemic of diphtheria, scarlet fever or poliomyelitis? The 1930's probably. Recalling this reminded me how rudimentary were the counter-procedures then.

I stood and watched as the postman delivering parcels pushed his large wicker basket on bicycle sized wheels. Even now – in 2017 – the presence of this equipment stirred a feeling of foreboding. Why was this? It was only an everyday figure going about his usual work. It took me a time to figure this out, but I am sure I know why now; so let's go back a long way in time – to the nineteen-thirties, in fact.

In 1937, I was eight years old. We lived in a small country town and it was here that I went to school. I still marvel that one lone teacher could take all thirty of us for most lessons. Arithmetic, geography, history, reading, writing – just about the lot. All that and she stayed smiling. Miss Aldred was her name. And we learned – well, at least I know that I did. After lessons, some of us would stay behind for sketching tutorials. She provided the paper and pencils for this and guided our attempts.

We were encouraged to make friends. I sat at the desk next to Nola and she and I got on well. We had started at the school at the same time and we soon found out that she liked many of the things I liked. A game of cricket in the meadow. Roaming the local woods looking for places to make our version of a camp. Picnics – paste sandwiches and a bottle of cold tea. In those days they called her a 'tomboy'. That wouldn't do today, would it?

Looking back at those days now I have to ask myself, *Was the sun always shining?* since it feels now that it was. I know when the sun stopped shining. But that was yet to come. If those days sounded too good to be true, I'm coming to what kicked this tale off. One of the events I hated was having to go shopping with my mother. This was always a trip to our High Street where she had the habit of suddenly crossing the road to avoid meeting someone coming towards us. This meant some relative with whom she was not on speaking terms was coming.

I had seen no-one that I knew and so I asked, "Why are we crossing now?"

"Look over there," and she pointed at a man in a boiler suit pushing a basket on bicycle-sized wheels. It was made of wicker work, had a hinged lid and was about six feet long. It was the first time I had seen anything like it.

"We have to get out of the way of it," she continued.

"Why?" I persisted. "He's not going to run us down. Is he?"

"It's a fumigation basket, and that means trouble for some poor soul, and stop asking questions."

I knew I wouldn't get any further, and Dad was always working late, so the following day I approached Miss Aldred's desk at break time. I told her what I had seen on the High Street. What she had to say caused me long-lasting dread, panic, horror – call it what you will. Diphtheria and scarlet fever, that was what it was all about, she told me. These were diseases of which I had never heard. I can't recall her exact descriptions but when she had finished, I knew these were highly contagious and what's more, they were certain killers. And the basket? It was wheeled through the streets to the home of anyone diagnosed as having either of these illnesses. Clothing and bedding were loaded into the basket, sprayed with a disinfectant, then wheeled away to be burnt. Before the man with the basket left the house he also sprayed the premises.

There was more. The person who had the disease was then likely to be sent to the Isolation Hospital at a little village some 5 miles away. I was later told that most who went there did not leave alive. The wheeled basket, the harbinger of death, it seemed to me then.

Weeks went by and the basket was no longer in the forefront of my mind. It was school holiday time and I went round to see if Nola was coming out to play. She lived many streets from our house on a very steep hill, far enough away that I had not seen her since the holidays started. Her mother answered the door. She told me that Nola was not well – a cold with a sore throat and she was staying in bed. A shame, really; I had thought we could go and make a camp from branches in the local wood. Now I would have to think of something else. And my cricket bat was busted!

A few days dragged by and I still hadn't found much to do, so I thought I would try Nola again. As I turned the corner of her street I saw the man with the basket, some way up the steep hill, straining to keep the basket moving in the summer heat. He had stopped outside number 32. Number 32 was where Nola lived. Oh no. No. No. She had been in bed with a sore throat. I hung back. I didn't want to get too close to the man. And then he wiped his face with his handkerchief and started pushing again. He stopped further up the hill. My best guess was it was outside number 44, though I couldn't be sure, and I wasn't going any closer. He wedged the basket against the kerb, pulled a cloth mask over his nose and knocked on the door. That was enough for me. I turned and ran home.

At the start of the new term I sat down at the desk next to Nola. With the new school year we had now gone up a class, and we were speculating about what our new teacher would be like. I thought about our first teacher when we started at this school.

"Won't be as good as Miss Aldred," I said. "Wish we could have her again."

Nola pulled a strange face.

"We won't be seeing her again. She's gone."

"What do you mean, she's gone?"

"She lived up the hill from us. Number 44. They took her to the Isolation."

Nola didn't need to say any more. I felt the pain in my stomach.

It was during the next summer holiday that I tried out my new bike. It wasn't exactly new, just new to me. Uncle Harry, who was a dustman, with one of those leather shoulder guards for hoisting dustbins up to the dust cart, had 'rescued' it from the Council Scrap Yard. He had done it up for me.

"New brake blocks, tyres and tubes," he had said. "Almost as good as new."

I called on Nola and we went off on our bikes on a sketching trip, (her bike *really* was new). We decided to go across the Common until we reached the escarpment looking out on the Aylesbury Plain. There below was a lovely little village which cried out to be drawn.

We propped our bikes up and started deciding on our subjects. Nola was quick to settle on the black and white pub with the duck pond and stocks in front of it. We argued whether it was too much for one sketch and then I spotted what I thought was the perfect scene. I was looking down on a red-tiled, single storied building with buff walls, set in a large plot which was covered in flowers – red, orange, white, with the occasional beds of blue or mauve. Around the whole area was a stone wall, which was probably higher than it seemed from the distance where we sat. It couldn't be a private house.

Nola leant over to look at the drawing I had started.

Wrinkling her nose, she said "You don't want to be drawing that."

"Why not? I like it better than your mouldy old pub."

"Don't you know? It's the Isolation."

"That's where Miss… "

"Yes."

All these years later, tucked away in a drawer at home, I still have the grubby, part-finished sketch of the single storey building with all the flowers. I never did finish it off with water colours.

At the bottom in scratchy writing are the letters, RIP.

THE CHRONICLES OF
GREAT UNCLE WILBUR

There is likely to be a Great Uncle Wilbur (or Great Aunt Wilhelmina for that matter) tucked away in most families – someone with similar characteristics, even if his or her physique is quite different.

Great Uncle Wilbur is just 5ft 2in tall, so in that respect he's not all that great, but to say he is eccentric is to understate the case. Not wildly madly eccentric; just a strong tendency to accident proneness. Most just nod and say, "That's Great Uncle Wilbur for you", though I am not so sure that that is how Great Aunt Martha sees it. I should mention, too, that Great Uncle seems to attract others who, even unwittingly, contribute to events. Foremost of these is Leslie Walkerton – known to everyone locally as 'Big Les' or 'Big Bird'. At 6ft 5ins, he dwarfs Great Uncle in every respect. There follow a few examples which should clarify what I mean.

1. A TUNE OR TWO FOR CHRISTMAS

Christmas was coming, and Great Uncle Wilbur was out of funds. Not to put too fine a point on it, he was skint. He felt he hadn't much to look forward to if he couldn't give a present or two to his younger relatives and so he was prepared to take advice wherever it might be found about how to raise his level of income.

He always looked to the regulars of the Shoemakers

Arms for advice and after an hour of heated discussion, while he supped his half pint of bitter, they came to a unanimous conclusion. The answer was busking – a public performance in the town centre's shopping mall. They reasoned that at this time of the year, people were generous beyond measure and such an enterprise couldn't fail. They also elicited the fact that many years before, Great Uncle had played the cornet in the town's silver band, though he had omitted to say that it was only on one occasion and that was before he was requested to leave to protect the band's reputation. The advice came quicker than Great Uncle could absorb. What remained in his mind when all was said was first, the busker must dress well – looking like a vagrant wasn't on – and second, having a dog with you increased your chances no end.

Big Les was the first to offer practical help. Since he played the melodeon with the Morris Men he claimed to know the ropes when it came to street performances.

"I'll come and get you under way," he promised.

On a wind-swept Saturday morning, Great Uncle arrived about nine-thirty at the chosen pitch, at the mouth of a small alleyway between two of the High Street stores and shivered as he waited for Big Les who loped into position ten minutes later. Great Uncle hadn't reckoned with Les wearing his Morris gear and at first he thought he was being savaged by Big Bird from TV's Sesame Street. Les has a long beaky nose and the most evident part of his dress was a full jacket festooned with small pieces of yellow cloth, sewn on to look like feathers. But before panic took over, the bells round the knees and the clogs gave the game away.

Not that Great Uncle wasn't distinctively attired himself. With the words 'dress well' imprinted in his mind. he had shaken the moth balls out of his hacking jacket with the tailored slit at the back. And with putty colour thermal long johns worn outside, giving the appearance of jodhpurs, and a pair of shiny black Wellington boots, he would have cut an imposing figure, had he been taller than five feet two inches. Round his neck was neatly tied the white silk scarf provided by Great Aunt Martha, with her old horseshoe charm brooch securing it. Topping the lot was the bowler he had bought for a funeral eighteen years before.

And what of the dog? Gladys, the Shoemakers landlady, had insisted Great Uncle should take her pet Corgi, a rusty coloured animal with sharp features and a cunning smile. Not that she was a pedigree or anything like that. According to some of the regulars, she was crossed with a ferret, but no matter. The dog shivered along with Great Uncle. Big Les always had a soft spot for animals – he kept newts as a youngster – so he fashioned a kennel from cardboard boxes found in the alley and the corgi settled in, poking its head out from time to time, to keep an eye on anyone muscling in on her territory.

They were ready to perform. Big Les had his top hat, decked with artificial flowers in true Morris style. He placed it crown down on the pavement. He only knew three tunes – all sounding remarkably like the 'Kerry Dance' – and he persisted with these, adding ribald words as a measure of variation. Great Uncle went through his whole repertoire, from 'Alpine Echoes' and 'Away in a Manger', to

'Zorba the Greek's Dance'.

By now, the spectacle of Big Bird's animated antics and Great Uncle's elegant cool, plus occasional enigmatic glimpses of the dog, had attracted a substantial crowd. The top hat was gathering a surprising sum of money and Big Les swooped now and again to clear it out. Having nowhere to put it in his outfit he had to stuff the takings into the pockets of Great Uncle's jacket. This manoeuvre brought rapturous applause from the crowd.

It was turned mid-day and Great Uncle was enjoying himself, but by now he had played his complete repertoire so many times he didn't know what he was blowing. How he lit upon 'D'you Ken John Peel', with a smart chorus of 'Tantivy, Tantivy, Tantivy', he would never know. Later he was to say it was fate, purely fate.

At that moment, from the Axe and Cleaver public house stepped Balaclava Brian, ready for the football, with most of the four pre-match pints he had consumed still inside him. A seasoned hunt saboteur, he was preoccupied with considering whether he should switch his energies from the hunting fraternity to anglers. Still sabotaging, of course. It was then that he became aware of the music. His eyes took in the almost life-size model of a horseman blowing hunting tunes. Provocation, that's what it was. Not only a model that played the hunting horn but there was a fox, a real live fox, at its side, with an appealing look that said, *Save me*. He reached up to pull his Balaclava into place, but all that he found was his beanie hat in his football team's colours. He felt naked, but a little thing like this would not stop him moving into action.

Great Uncle was transported as he played, oblivious, eyes shut. Big Les, though, senses sharpened from his street experiences with the Morris Men, spotted the intruder. It must be an attempt to snatch his coin-laden hat and from his sash he drew the stout stick used in some of the dances, where a performer whacks another's stick, hoping to avoid cracking anything important.

The dog was alerted by this defensive action and sneaked, leering, towards the front of its makeshift kennel, crouching, back up, tail rigid. As Balaclava Brian bounced forward she howled, a yelp meant to warn him to keep his distance, but he misread the signal.

"You little beauty, I'll save you," he yelled, as he flung himself nearer. Big Les did three steps of the 'Boxing Day Mummer's Dance' and brought the stick down on Brian's back, felling him. The interloper's ample backside caught the dog on its nose and with such an affront it leapt forward and sank its teeth into the rounded buttocks. The crowd was ecstatic. But however it was viewed, judging by the amount of money going into the hat, its entertainment value rated highly.

At this point, round the corner trod Constable Wellbeloved. He had been alerted on his radio of a disturbance in the shopping mall but the cheering and booing, as though a pantomime was in full stride, wasn't what he expected. Events had overtaken Great Uncle, too. He was now out of the trance-like state and was staring around, a man bemused. He stretched and raised his cornet to his lips and in this defenceless position was an easy target for PC Wellbeloved, whose six feet five inches blocked what little light there was – a veritable giant to Jack atop the beanstalk.

Then of a sudden, the constable came to a standstill. The crowd hushed. Drama, as all the best football commentators aver. That's what it was, real drama. No-one present suspected that PC Wellbeloved had only the previous day completed a human relations course and now the instructor's words were working their way through his mind –

"Wellbeloved, at six feet five inches tall you're likely to intimidate the average man or woman. Put yourself in a position where you sort of... shrink a bit, know what I mean? Come down to their level."

This was the first opportunity he had had to put the lesson into practice and here was the very person to practice on. He lowered himself onto one knee and was looking straight into Great Uncle Wilbur's eyes.

"Give her a kiss!" came the cry. Then, "Tell 'im you can't, little 'un. You're already spoken for!"

In the turmoil of the moment, PC Wellbeloved forgot the sort of words that should go with the posture. What he actually said was, "I'll have you, you snipped-off little garden gnome!"

Great Uncle was confused. So far, the day had gone beyond his expectations, with the money flowing in, but now there was this commotion all around him. And what was the policeman doing staring at him. He looked to his right and there was the dog still shaking its head violently while holding on to Balaclava Brian. Big Les continued to belabour him with his Morris stick and uncle could see that he was in danger of being blamed for all this.

Suddenly, recognising the absurd position he was in, PC Wellbeloved drew himself to his full height. Great Uncle took his chance. Clutching his cornet, he dived between the constable's legs and the crowd opened up for his passage like the Red Sea for Moses. Seeing her surrogate master making off, the dog took her teeth out of Brian's backside and sped after Great Uncle.

The representative of the law was in danger of losing even more face, so he turned to pursue Great Uncle and the dog, but he hadn't the power of a biblical patriarch. Eventually he struggled through the crowd, which had closed even tighter, but there was no sight of his quarry. The shopping crowd was deeper now and he barely noticed the lad in the sandy coloured Davey Crocket hat riding the slot machine horse at one side of the arcade.

"Gone like magic," the constable complained to himself, as he eased his flak jacket, adjusted his belt laden with hardware, removed his helmet and scratched his head.

Great Uncle dismounted the horse at the end of his second fifty-pence-worth. One turn on the horse would have been enough to evade the law but he had been enjoying the ride too much to end it then. The dog jumped down from where it had been crouching on his head. With the foxy creature at his heel, he made his way to the Shoemakers to return her to her owner.

"Sweet-natured little love, isn't she," crooned Gladys. "What sort of day did you have?"

What could Great Uncle say? How do you measure a busker's day? He felt his pockets sagging with the weight of the coins, but he still felt the cold in the marrow of his bones. To his mind the one balanced the other.

"All right, really. Half of bitter please."

2. WILBUR'S FISHY ADVENTURE

Great Uncle is an avid reader and Ernest Hemingway's 'Old Man and the Sea' made such an impression on him, that he was inspired to do whatever he could to have a similar experience as the old man in the story. You will recall that in this, the old man was towed around the ocean by the monarch of all marlins. Since we live as far from the sea as is possible in England, there aren't many marlins around here, but he lit on a passable alternative when he went for his nightly half pint of bitter in the Shoemakers Arms.

The town's angling club was meeting and their usual conversation about the relative merits of coloured or plain maggots was overtaken by talk of a monster pike in Two Mile Lake. Big Les swore that he had seen it take a full-grown duck in one swipe. Maybe the fish was not marlin size, but in the coarse fisherman's parlance it was stonking big. Great Uncle continued to eavesdrop and two conditions for enticing big fish to the hook became clear – one was 'the bigger the fish the bigger the bait' and the other was 'a successful piker always dresses ugly'. No-one made clear what dressing ugly was like, so it was open to Great Uncle to interpret this in his own fashion.

From the attic, he rescued the old rod and tackle he

hadn't used for years, booked the rowing boat at the lake, and collected plump sardines and a fresh herring for bait from a supermarket. Dressing ugly was no problem. His old gabardine raincoat, tied round with a bit of sash cord to replace the lost belt, and a pair of wellies that the dog had chewed, fitted the bill. Great Aunt Martha shook her head and said he looked like a bag of manure tied in the middle.

His Hemingway expedition – as he called it – started at crack of dawn. At the end of the car park, where he left his bike, is a wheelie bin. Its inside was always cool, and knowing it was not yet due for emptying, into it he popped half his fish bait for safe keeping. Also, the bin was seldom used, most people preferring a more liberal approach to rubbish disposal. If he needed more bait he could always come back and retrieve this portion and if he didn't need more, it was there for his tea.

After four hours, his fantasy of being towed by a giant fish was coming true. He lost all his bait to bites which sent the float scudding around all over the lake, as though it had a life of its own. Now he had to collect the rest of his bait, if he wasn't to miss the adventure of a lifetime. He rowed back to the bank, took his wellies off and left them in the boat since they were uncomfortable for walking, and made his way in his army surplus grey socks to the bin. As you know, Great Uncle is short and wheelie bins are deep and reaching for the bottom of the wheelie bin was a task for which he was not physically fitted.

At this time, taking their constitutional, was a couple whose joint image radiated benevolence and good works. As one, they spotted the dirty grey socks waving in the air, the rest of Great Uncle's person being inside the wheelie bin. They were bemused until the rest emerged, clutching a large herring in the right hand. Strands of cabbage garlanded his hair and his greying stubble was a nest for broken eggshells.

"You poor man, having to scavenge for your food," they bewailed in unison, sounding not unlike the beginning of a Gregorian chant.

She looked at her husband. "He must have a square meal, Arthur. If we give him money he will only spend it on… "

She couldn't let the word pass her lips.

"Yes dear. We'll take him to the place round the corner."

They hauled Great Uncle out of the bin and, with one either side holding him by his elbows, they escorted him to Mr Hung Lo's chippie. At their bidding, a large plate of haddock and chips was brought and placed on the only table in the shop. For one so small, Great Uncle has a surprisingly deep voice at the best of times, like the rumbling of an elephant's interior, and when perturbed it's an octave lower, so his protest was mistaken for other bodily noises. With a firm hand his head was pushed down – like they do in those TV programmes when the police put a suspect in the back of a car – and his backside landed heavily on the hard metal chair, cracking the miniature of whisky in his hip pocket, there because if the surrogate marlin lasted until the evening, Great Uncle might need warming.

The odour of the spirit was barely detectable to the

average nose, but it hit his Lady Bountiful's taste buds like an oil slick from a distressed tanker washing over a nature reserve.

"Well, we should have known better, Arthur, we should have guessed," and nose in the air, with her husband in tow, she bustled from the shop, leaving Wilbur stranded.

Great Uncle's relief turned to panic when Mr. Lo demanded payment. He stood up and turned his empty pockets inside out to demonstrate his inability to meet the bill. The only response from the chippie was to disappear behind the counter to reappear waving a chopper, which caused Great Uncle to flee the shop as fast as his socks would take him.

Within a few yards of the door, he ran straight into six feet five inches of Constable Wellbeloved.

"Thank goodness," rumbled Great Uncle. "Saved by the law."

As is the way of the world, the constable made the natural assumption – at least to him – that this scruffy unwashed had been doing the unthinkable; abusing Mr Lo.

"You're nicked for racial abuse," declared Wellbeloved, and Great Uncle was marched off to the police station in handcuffs.

Nothing newsworthy normally happens in the town, certainly nothing meriting space at ten o'clock at night on the television. So it was, that Great Aunt Martha pricked her ears up when the town's name was associated with a rowing boat found adrift on Two Mile Lake. The camera zoomed in on a pair of chewed wellies, standing forlornly in the stern of the craft, and then switched to the police underwater search team.

"Could it be accident, suicide or even... *murder?*"

The newscaster lowered her voice, tremolo, as she asked the question.

"Stuff and nonsense!" snorted Great Aunt, and made her way to the police station, though she didn't foresee the consequence of this for Great Uncle Wilbur. Forthwith a charge of wasting police time was slapped on him.

The fickleness of fortune is illustrated by the next turn of events. Months later, all spruced up, with stubble removed, and in his best suit, Great Uncle went to court for the hearing. At first it all went wrong, when a short-sighted probation officer popped a sweet into Great Uncle's mouth, took him by the hand and led him into the juvenile court, but hours later when the error was recognised, he stood before the magistrates, his hat in his hands.

It is remarkable that he is probably the only accused person to have his case dismissed due to a gale in the English Channel. Benefiting from some bizarre regulations and creative rostering on the part of his superiors, Constable Wellbeloved commutes to his duties monthly from Normandy. The storms along the channel disrupted all the ferry timetables, PC Wellbeloved was twenty-four hours late for the hearing, and the case was dismissed for lack of evidence.

Great Uncle Wilbur sits before the fireside gripped by the 'The Finer Points of Snake Charming', a graphically illustrated early edition by an anonymous Indian author.

"Don't even entertain the thought!" wailed Great Aunt Martha, as she visualised a hooded cobra emerging from her washing basket.

3. THE INSTRUMENT FROM OZ

The letter from nephew Jake invited Great Uncle Wilbur to a party. For the outlay of £10, Jake had emigrated to Australia in 1956. And now here he was in England on holiday, inviting great uncle to a get-together. Wilbur hardly remembered Jake, but his curiosity caused him to accept the invitation. He spruced himself up and caught a bus that would take him close to where Jake was staying. Great Aunt Martha recalled Jake only too well and declined the invitation.

As the party came to an end, Jake handed out presents. Soft toy kangaroos, koalas and duck-billed platypuses, and wooden hand-painted boomerangs were pulled from a large bag and given out to cousins, nephews, aunts and uncles.

The bag was now empty and Great Uncle felt over-looked until Jake said, "And for my favourite uncle a special present. Knowing his love of music, I thought an instrument was in order."

From behind the settee he produced a five feet long hollowed out tree branch, decorated with rings of red ochre and a multitude of coloured beads laid into the wood in mystic patterns.

"You know what it is, of course? It's a didgeridoo," explained Jake.

It was like no instrument Great Uncle had ever encountered, but always gracious, he beamed and gave his thanks.

It was time to go home. Jake produced a large sheet of thick brown wrapping paper, which was secured round the present by generous lengths of adhesive parcel tape. Great Uncle set off home carrying the bundle, which was nearly as long as he was tall. Having missed the last bus, he started to walk home and the nearer he was to his house the more tired he became. He hoisted the bundle onto his shoulder to ease the burden.

Meanwhile, around the corner in a quiet side road, PC Wellbeloved sat in a police car. He watched, startled and then puzzled, as the shadow fell on a wall along the road in front of him – a figure striding purposefully, with a long object on his shoulder. Now what did that remind him of? Instantly, into his mind came the warnings of his inspector to keep a weather eye open for possible terrorists. It could happen here, not just in London, had been the sharp reminder.

Now our valiant law enforcer was in two minds. Get out of the warm car and go and check this man and be faced with at least twenty minutes of filling in forms, when he was just about to go off duty. Or ignore the incident. The spectre of form filling held him in its grip until his sense of duty got the upper hand. Yes, it did look like a rocket launcher the man was carrying. There would be no forms for that.

He radioed for instructions.

"Back Lane. Man probably carrying rocket launcher."

The answer was swift. Wellbeloved was to keep the individual in sight and back-up would be there forthwith.

No sooner had he crept round the corner, than a screeching of vehicles stopping came from each end of the road. A flood light had picked out the figure with the object on his shoulder and he had stopped in his tracks. In fact, so suddenly had he stopped that the parcel shot off his shoulder and landed in the road a yard or two in front of him. Coloured plastic incident tape appeared with remarkable speed, stretched across each end of Back Lane.

It so happened that Big Les, aka Big Bird, had been performing at a Morris Men function the other side of the town. He was still in his flamboyant dancing gear, bells jangling and ribbons fluttering, as he pedalled, head down breathing heavily, towards Back Lane on his way home. It was dark at his end of the Lane and such heavy weather was he making of the ride, that he failed to see the incident tape stretched across the road. It was the surprise of it engaging with his mouth rather than its strength that caused him to tumble from his bicycle. The din of the bells round his knees as they hit the tarmac and the oaths he uttered caused a police constable who was sitting inside a van nearby to sit up and take notice.

"You can't go down there. There's a major incident on."

"Who stuck that stuff across a public thoroughfare without giving ample warning? I could have done myself fatal damage."

"We did. There's an incident on."

"That won't stop me taking a civil action against your Chief Constable. Gross negligence is what it is. I'm associated with Huckster and Huckster."

He saw no harm in stretching the truth; he delivered the free newspaper to the solicitors each week.

"Who's in charge here?"

The constable knew the law firm and its reputation, and he also knew his Superintendent's annoyance with claims against the police.

"The Inspector's down at the incident."

"You'd better take me to him, then," and Big Les disentangled himself from the plastic tape, scooped up his bike, straightened the handlebars and set off towards the bright lights at the other end of Back Lane.

The constable had little option but to follow in his wake, keeping sufficient distance to avoid being associated with this curiously dressed individual. As Big Les came near to the floodlight, he could see the small body lying face down on the pavement, ringed at a distance by armed police. He was sure he recognised the figure.

An authoritarian voice cut through the night.

"I say again, what's the object you discarded in front of you?"

This had left Great Uncle in confusion. He is a precise sort of man, certain he hadn't discarded anything. It had flown from his shoulder when he was stopped so peremptorily. Catching the sight of the guns out of the corner of his eye he thought he had better say something.

"It's a didgeridoo."

"Cor, a didgeridoo! Second generation Australian land

to air missile tested at Woomera in 1970"

This aside by a jack-the-lad constable was meant as a joke. There was no way anyone would take him seriously, was there? On the contrary, the reaction was the sharp sound of firearms being loaded.

Big Les had now identified the shrinking figure on the pavement as Great Uncle. He also knew a didgeridoo when he saw one, even though wrapped in brown paper, and you might well ask what self-respecting Morris Man wouldn't know one. Oblivious to the fact that the scene resembled Manet's painting of the execution of Emperor Maximillian, he strode forward, bells jingling, ribbons fluttering and clogs clack-clack-clacking.

Swiftly he stripped the instrument of its covering. He held the naked branch aloft.

"Look!" he yelled, the instrument's inlaid beads shining in the beam of light.

No response from the marksmen. He lowered the didgeridoo until it was resting on the ground, bent over and put his mouth to it and blew. The sound that emerged was later likened to the death throes of the Titanic.

"Now do you believe me? And the little chap is Wilbur. Everyone knows Wilbur. Don't you Mr. Wellbeloved?"

This addressed to the tall constable who was already slinking back to his car.

The guns were lowered, shoulders slumped, the piercing light was extinguished and there was the sound of the posse withdrawing. Great Uncle had by now risen to his feet and was dusting himself down, when a police officer stepped forward.

"Do you know the trouble you've caused? In future you want to watch what you are doing. And get that lump of wood out of here before we do you for littering."

He turned and left with the rest of the police.

Big Les helped Great Uncle up on the crossbar of his bike and – a little wobbly – together they rode off into the night. The primitive instrument that had been at the root of Great Uncle's brush with the law stuck out in front of the cycle like the proboscis of some extinct animal, casting an even more alarming shadow than the one that swung PC Wellbeloved into action.

It was late when Great Uncle reached home and he climbed the stairs gingerly, not wishing to wake Great Aunt Martha. Though well intended, these efforts were unnecessary. Great Aunt was sitting up in bed reading.

"Well, there you are, Wilbur. You're awfully late, but at least I've had the chance to finish my book. It's all about spies and awful weapons on the streets of a country town. Very exciting but very far-fetched. Could you imagine it happening here?"

"No, dear, I can't imagine it. but I'm sure there are people who could."

4. OSCILLATING PLUMBITIS

Great Uncle Wilbur had never had a day off work for sickness in his life and the fact that he woke up one morning, with his body refusing to get out of bed, and a dullness in his heart that he hadn't felt before, shook him to the core. Eventually Great Aunt Martha persuaded him to see the doctor and this caused him even greater anxiety.

Doctor William McNally put away his blood pressure equipment and said, "Stress. You've been overdoing it Mr. Appleby."

"What can you give me for it?"

"Nothing, Mr. Appleby. Nothing. What you need is a diversion, a relaxing diversion. Something that will take you out of yourself, something you haven't done recently for preference. No going back to work just yet."

This didn't sound to Great Uncle as much of a medical opinion, but he wasn't one to argue; he was of an age that still gave the medical profession respect.

That evening he met Big Les in the Shoemakers Arms for his daily half pint of bitter. He told him of his meeting with the doctor and ended, "I don't know what to do. What does he mean by a diversion?"

Big Les thought for a moment.

"Didn't you tell me once that your granddad's golf clubs are up in the attic? There's no better diversion. Nothing too athletic, needs a bit of concentration, but a walk with purpose across the countryside, breathing in all that lovely fresh air will do you no end of good."

"But I don't know how to play."

"Nothing to it. I'll teach you. You'll cotton on in no time."

His enthusiasm caused him to forget that it took himself many long hours before he could hit the ball with accuracy any distance at all.

And that was the start of it. Great Uncle fetched down the clubs, dusted them off and showed them to Big Les.

"They're a little on the old side," said his friend, playing down the fact that no-one had seen a hickory shafted brassie or niblick on a course for over a hundred years. "But they'll do while you get the hang of it."

The local municipal course had no driving range. After practice swings in the garden, they were straight out onto the first fairway. Two hours later they had arrived on the fourth tee after a series of zigzags from rough to rough across the first three fairways.

Big Les was never one to acknowledge defeat, nor to admit that he could possibly be wrong.

"You've got the makings. Another couple of rounds and you'll be a new man."

Four days later, they were on the first tee again. Great Uncle's progress was much the same as the first time. He shifted large clods of earth and grass, but the ball had generally stayed close to him. When the next attempt at the game was made, his anxiety level was patently soaring. Big Les knew he had to do something. Quickly. Some said he had the scruples of a three-card trickster but what he was about to do was justified, since it was for Great Uncle's well-being. With a bag of second hand clubs he visited the backstreet workshop of Sparky. Sparky knew his way around the world of technology so intimately, the Shoemakers Arms intelligentsia held that he could have engineered his own moon landing, had he the backing.

At crack of dawn the next Monday morning, ignoring

the notices that said no ball games other than football, Big Les tried the clubs out on the village soccer ground. More than satisfied with their performance he called for Wilbur and steered him to the sports field. He put a ball on a tee and selected a club generally used for short distances.

"Nice and steady now. Aim for the goal post. It's about 50 yards," he said.

Great Uncle took a deep breath. Was he in for another heaped helping of humiliation? He swung the club and the ball landed ten yards to the right of his target.

While he was mouthing to himself, "I'm stopping while I'm ahead," Big Les had taken the club from him and with a small screwdriver was turning a screw at the bottom of the club's shaft. He dragooned the reluctant Wilbur into making another shot. This time there was a metallic clunk as the ball hit the goal post. With the same procedure Great Uncle used all the clubs in the bag with what any golfer would recognise as unbelievable results. He, of course, knew no better; he only felt relief that he could now continue with the therapy prescribed by his doctor.

As the pair set out again for the Municipal course, Big Les decided he would look out of place alongside Wilbur's new found prowess.

"This bag's too big for you. I'll caddy until we can get you a trolley," he announced.

The only caddy Wilbur had ever known was the one in which Great Aunt Martha kept the tea but he kept quiet for fear of showing his ignorance. The little man's first drive travelled two hundred and twenty yards and was in the middle of the fairway. Big Les selected a club and Wilbur's next shot landed on the green, three feet from the flag marking the hole into which the ball should now go. Big Les passed the putter and Great Uncle smacked the ball. I say 'smacked', since the ball was so close to the hole that only a gentle tap that was necessary. It flew off the green and landed in the long grass. Big Les gulped. It was the only club Sparky had not addressed. No matter, they could continue the round, and maybe he could school Wilbur into not using the putter with such zest. Wilbur drove off at the tenth hole. Half way round the course and, the putts aside, he was making the kind of progress that one normally only sees on television big match coverage.

McNally and a fellow medico also enjoyed a round of golf. They had decided to play at the Municipal course, since they were pushed for time and it was handier than their usual venue, the plush County Club. They started at the tenth tee, from which Great Uncle had already driven his ball. He groaned as Wilbur took his stance for his second shot at the ball that was in the middle of the fairway. He was going to be held up all the way. That's the worst thing about these Municipals. The man stood like a complete novice, waggled his club as though he were a coarse fisherman landing a minnow and... and... and hit the ball straight onto the green, a hundred and fifty yards away.

Luck. Beginner's fortune. Look at the putt, for Heaven's sake. Three feet from the hole and he smacks it off into the rough. Hasn't a clue. As the two doctors came off the green, having each made a satisfying one over par, they heard the thwack of a ball being hit from the next tee.

They couldn't believe their eyes. McNally recognised the little man returning the driver to the bag. Mr. Appleby. His ball was dead centre of the fairway, at least two hundred and fifty yards from the tee. McNally decided they would keep as close behind the pair in front at a distance where he could watch this remarkable golf. And that was the way Great Uncle finished his 18 holes. Immaculate shots until he putted.

McNally and his companion settled down for a drink in the bar of the Municipal course.

"You seem to know the short man… " said McNally's companion.

"Oh, indeed I do. He's a patient of mine. Hadn't seen him for years, until a few weeks ago. I diagnosed stress and said he should go and find a diversion. The way he plays it looks as though he's been working on that diversion for years. In the Pro's shop they say he has only been coming on Tuesdays for the past three weeks. You don't become that good in a few weeks."

His companion nodded his agreement.

"But his swing! Have you ever seen anything like it? There's something strange about this."

And so McNally decided to see what happened on the following Tuesday.

And on Tuesday, there they were on the first tee, short golfer and his lengthy caddy. McNally and his inquisitive companion followed them at a distance where they could witness every stroke. At the end of 18 holes they were still non-plussed. Par for the course was 65 and the little man had completed it in 60. Even his putting had been miraculously on target. This was the sort of a round big-time professionals played.

McNally and his fellow medico again retired to the bar.

"Well, what do you think, William? Have you solved this mystery?"

"I wish I could say I have," said McNally. "No-one with such a wretched golf swing could achieve what the little man was doing, without working on it for many years. So, that aside, I have made a decision."

"And what is that?"

"I shall call him in to my surgery and tell him to get back to work as soon as he can. It looks to me as though he has engineered an absence from work to indulge his passion for golf. And I have aided and abetted this... I shall give him a medical certificate to take to his employer... "

"Yes?"

"And the certificate will say 'Oscillating plumbitis.'

"That's a new one on me."

"Let's leave it at that for now, shall we?"

Big Les waited in the Shoemakers Arms until Great Uncle appeared.

"What did the doc have to say?"

"Not much. Nothing wrong really. Said I should go back to work. He gave me a medical certificate."

Great Uncle fished in his pocket and placed a piece of paper on the table in front of Big Les. The words *'Oscillating Plumbitis',* in large black print, hit Big Les in the eye.

"Have you ever come across that complaint?" asked Great Uncle.

Despite a carefully cultivated image Big Les was, as they used to say, something of a scholar.

"No. No. Never."

No way was he going to upset Great Uncle by telling his all-trusting friend the part he had played in getting him into this position.

He certainly wasn't going to explain that *Oscillating Plumbitis* meant *Swinging the Lead* .

ADAM'S LONG NIGHT

Most ghost stories are fashioned from the imagination. Few are prompted by a real experience, even if sceptics denounce this experience as imagination. Here's a story which certainly did not come from my imagination. See what you think. All names have been changed for the sake of anonymity.

The 5-day management course I contracted to tutor was to be held in a small hotel in a Cotswolds village. The venue had been chosen by the MD of the company, since he had stayed there and liked the place. Even so, he asked me to look it over to see that it not only met the social requirements of his managers, but had all the necessary facilities for this type of training.

I also liked what I saw. It was homely and the staff appeared friendly and helpful. It was originally a coaching inn but had undergone some development to increase the accommodation. Some of the original bedrooms were still in existence; the remainder came from extending the hotel in the 1980s.

The first day of the programme went well. The 15 course members settled in quickly and were motivated enough to carry on working after dinner. Since they came from several different company locations, they had taken a little time to get to know each other, but a few drinks soon changed this for the majority. One person did stand out from the rest, however. Adam Greenway. Adam was an accountant in the Finance Department at the company's head office and by the end of the evening, I was not alone in noting his formality. Attempts to bring him into the evening's activities by his course mates fell flat.

I had been made aware of his temperament by the company's Training Manager, who told me that one of the hopes of the MD was that Adam would become more responsive to others. An important figure in Finance, his personality left him isolated and this had a negative effect on the Department. A tall order; five days is not long for this kind of change to be achieved, but I can fairly say that I had managed such a change in past courses. I could hope.

The second day was much the same and the third and fourth even better; except for Adam Greenway. Whereas the rest of the course members were digging deep into the work, he was only playing at it. I am not naïve enough to believe that everyone who comes on a management course – particularly one involving behavioural change – does so of their own volition and welcomes it.

Dinner was treated as a special occasion, being the last evening of the course. Conversation was lively. A few asides were thrown around – among them the customary 'bean counter' jokes, especially from those who had to deal with Greenway in their normal duties. After the evening session had finished, the group made its way to the bar; some played darts and other pub games. I had notes to make and left them to it, but when I returned about 10.30, I was told that Adam had disappeared earlier, no-one having seen the going of him. This was now troubling me, since the only change in Adam had been to isolate himself. I went to bed with some misgivings.

On courses of this nature I always came to breakfast early, in case there was someone who wanted a quiet word before any others appeared. To my surprise Adam Greenway appeared shortly after I arrived. Although I was the only person at the long table set out for the whole course, he sat on his own at the end. I greeted him but there was no acknowledgement. I looked closer at him. He didn't look well, and since he drank little it wasn't a hangover. I can only say he 'looked grey'. I moved my place close to where he was sitting.

"Adam, aren't you feeling well?"

As I asked the question, more of his colleagues arrived and he turned away from me and carried on moving his cereal around in the bowl.

I felt I could not leave it there. I wasn't sure what to do, but Adam made my mind up for me. Abruptly he turned to me and said quietly, "I want a word with you."

He nodded towards the conservatory and, dropping his serviette onto the table, made off. When I reached the conservatory, he had picked a spot out of the view of his course colleagues.

"I don't know how to tell you about something that happened, but I thought you ought to know."

I let him continue.

"I can't take socialising, so I went to bed early, especially since it's a long journey home. Short of reading matter, I started looking at your hand-out material in bed."

Did I spot a smile? Was he going to complain about my written notes? But no. Now the greyness was coming back. He carried on.

111

"I must have fallen asleep reading. The next thing I knew I was awake. There was a dull glow in the room – I couldn't tell where it came from. I felt cold, shivering. And then I saw a person. It looked like a young woman standing on the far side of the room. I thought, *it's one of those jokers from the course, taking the mickey.* I called out, 'I have to admit you're realistic. Where did you get the dress?' She was wearing a floral print dress, sort of 1920s/30s style. Definitely not one you'd be able to buy today."

I had never heard Adam speak so long before.

"She started moving towards the bed. I called out, 'You've had your bit of fun, now pack it in. Go to bed.' But she kept on coming. It was only when she was at the foot of the bed I saw the knife she was carrying."

He stopped; now he was really reliving the moment.

"I was scared out of my wits. And she started moving again, reaching out with the knife. I threw one pillow at her. Then another. She just dematerialised, if that's the right word."

He looked up at me; I think he was trying to judge if I believed what he had told me. For a man who was extremely judgemental and dismissive of anything that could not be proved, he had related the incident in terms that made me sure he believed what he had seen.

"You look better than when we came in," I said. "How do you feel now?"

"Better than I did. I'm glad you didn't sneer at what I had to say."

I don't think 'Thank you' was in his vocabulary.

"Will it help if you set off home as soon as you can? If

you want more help, I'll call in at your office in a week or two to discuss my notes."

He nodded and, as I started the first session, I saw through the window that he was driving off.

The course ended early and they were all gone. What Adam Greenway had told me had taken over my mind. I went out to the receptionist who I knew had been at the hotel for a long time. I chatted a little in answer to her questions about the course and then I said, "I wondered if any of your guests have ever reported anything strange happening."

"Such as?" she said.

Not wanting to give too much away I said, "Oh, just anything, anything unusual."

"Not that I can recall. Nothing in particular."

"Do you happen to have anything written about the history of the hotel? It must go back a long way."

"We don't have anything here, but I'm told Mrs. Gordon in the village Tourist Office has something. I've never seen it, though."

I was ready to leave, so I called in at the Tourist Office on my way home. Mary Gordon took some time to find what I wanted, saying no-one had enquired about it for years. I sat down in a quiet corner and read. The first few pages were pretty tame routine historical stuff. I almost gave up. but then, on the seventh page, I came upon it. The hair on the back of my neck prickled.

In 1927 the police had been called to the hotel in the early hours of the morning. In one of the bedrooms, a woman in her late twenties, Mildred by name, had been found dying; both her wrists had been sliced and a boning knife from the kitchen had been found on the floor near her.

There was more. She worked at the hotel and was known to have a lover – probably a commercial traveller – who stayed at the hotel each week. His body, with multiple stab wounds, was on the bed, which was soaked with his blood.

Did Adam Greenway know of this? I couldn't see how he could. What about his course mates? None came from this area and no-one had looked at the history of the hotel for years. I could only come to the obvious conclusion.

The story has a finale, I'm glad to say. The company Training Manager always reviews a course with each individual. A month had gone by and she asked me to go and see her. She gave me details of the feedback she had received and, after we had discussed this, she pushed back her chair and smiled.

"The MD has asked me to tell you about Adam."

Here It comes, I thought, expecting to have to defend some negatives.

"He says he didn't expect the course to have any effect on Adam. He just hoped it might do something, but the change seems to have run quite deep. The MD has no doubt that Adam's handling of people has changed for the better. He tried to push Adam to open up but all he would say was, 'I learnt something from reading the course notes in bed.'"

WHAT DID YOU DO... ?

Autobiography sounds a little ponderous, but I suppose that is what this next piece is. I am sometimes asked "What it was like, what did you do... growing up during the war; in the immediate post war years; living in Africa", and so on. At times I wonder – particularly if it is any of our grandchildren asking – if they think dinosaurs still roamed in those times.

I was born in Berkhamsted, which was then a small market town in Hertfordshire, 30 miles West of London. In 1942, I was 13 or so, and some of the lads from school had been riding their bikes near Bovingdon, a village about five miles from our town. They were breathless.

"Have you seen what's happening? The Yanks are levelling off the hills there and building a bomber 'drome," said one of them. "Someone said Liberators will be flying from there."

A few weeks or so later, they were. Was I excited? Well, yes, of course I was. What thirteen-year-old wouldn't be? I got on my bike and went to have a look.

But the real excitement came a month or two later, when we found they had based the American Forces Network radio station there. I was just beginning to listen to jazz and swing music, on gramophone records swapped with school mates. The war-time shops had negligible stocks, so we had to circulate the few we had. The BBC didn't acknowledge there was music called jazz or swing – dance bands and the Radio Rhythm Club (playing a watered-down version of Benny Goodman) were the best we could expect from our national broadcaster. Now, with the blessed AFN, we had two-hour-long sessions of the kind of music we had only dreamed about – all with disc jockeys; we'd never heard of these.

And the music! Louis Armstrong, Count Basie, Duke Ellington, Chick Webb, Benny Goodman, Artie Shaw, Harry James, Tommy Dorsey, Bunny Berigan, and a whole host more. Our whole world had changed. If you've not heard of these bands, I've no doubt they can be found on the internet – worth a listen.

I left school in 1946 aged 16. I loved cricket and joined Berkhamsted Town Club. The war had just ended, and servicemen were coming home. Many of them wanted the cricket they had promised themselves while they had been away. One ground, sixty or so players. Not much chance for a sixteen-year-old. A game every other week in the second XI, if lucky.

On a wet Sunday afternoon, with a match that never started, five of us stood together sheltering under the canopy of a tobacconist's shop in the centre of the town. (I even remember who we were; a former Army Sgt. Major, an ex-RAF pilot, a former Royal Navy rating, and myself and another boy, fresh from school). Like any small town, it was completely dead. No supermarkets then, no High Street shops open, and a few corner shops having off-licences opened for a short time on Sunday evenings.

We decided to form a Sunday wandering side from the club, to play local villages. No mobile phones. Private telephones were rare, but there were public phone boxes, none vandalized. Getting a village fixture secretary from the middle of a harvest field at 9.00 pm was part of the business and it proved difficult to do. Phone numbers were hard to trace and, more often than not, it meant a cycle ride into areas with which I wasn't familiar, to find the right person.

We had our first games. Transport was a problem. There were few car owners then. And there was petrol rationing, anyhow. Cycling and walking were the only options. Until along came David. His mother ran a farm in Tanganyika and as a visitor to Britain with a car, he was allowed more than the normal petrol ration. The car was an open Bristol sports car and we packed many more players in than it was designed for.

Our first match was at a village 12 miles or so from Berkhamsted. With the car overflowing, there were three of us on bikes hanging on to tow ropes, clutching cricket gear as best we could. No traffic, no police to speak of. And no Health and Safety legislation. Our 'Wanderers' side was up and running in style.

In most of the villages within a 20-mile radius of our town, cricket was an important part of social life. Even in those times when food and other rationing was in force, most villages competed to see who could lay on the best cricket tea. To us 'townies' it was a revelation to see what these farming communities could do. Jam made with strawberries from the farm and sugar produced from the farmer's own sugar beet crop was a special treat.

That was growing up in a small town in the 40s. In the 50s, I started an entirely different sort of life. On demobilisation from the Army in 1949, I rejoined the Hertfordshire Constabulary. I was stationed in the county's only city, St. Albans. Life was dull there. Britain was held down by austerity such as we have never seen since then. But a major factor for discontent was the conditions under which constables worked. Three shifts: 6.00 am to 2.00 pm, 2.00 pm to 10.00 pm, and 10.00 pm to 6.00 am. Seven days followed by one day off. One week-end off every seven weeks! Out on the streets for seven and a half hours. If you were lucky to have the city centre beat on nights, there was a bus depot, a snooker hall above Burtons the Tailors and a baker or two. The significance of these to a police patrolman was they had tea, hot steaming tea. But apart from very few occasions, this beat was retained for one of the older, longer served bobbies. The freshly appointed, like me, were given the outside beats, semi rural, which often meant walking long boring miles each shift.

One diversion, at least, was playing for the force rugby side. I had played against one of the Metropolitan Police divisions in the afternoon and was back on night duty at 10.00 pm. During the game, I had both my thumbs kicked back as I held the ball, and 'shaking hands with doorknobs' – that is, checking that shop doors were secure – was painful. It was pouring with rain when I went in to the station for my break at 1.30 am. In what passed for a canteen, we had to make our own tea and while I was eating the sandwiches my landlady supplied, I looked at the Police Review, our trade journal. There was a page full of adverts for Assistant Inspectors in Malaya, Cyprus, Tanganyika, and Kenya. And Inspectors in Uganda. All of these were open to application by constables in British Police forces. I opted for Uganda and my application went off the following day, more in hope than expectation.

A few weeks later, I was called to an interview at the Crown Agents for the Colonies in London. The interview ended, and I was asked if I had any questions. It had puzzled me how a 21-year-old could be appointed to the rank of Inspector, presumably over African ranks of longer service. The answer was that the Uganda Government wanted to seed the force with young officers who had been brought up in the British police ethic. (Perhaps a rather different ethic then than is to be found in Britain today!)

That still stuck in my mind, when a few years later, a very good African detective said, "When I arrest someone, why do I have to tell him he doesn't need to say anything unless he wishes to do so? It stops him confessing."

I don't think he found my explanation very convincing. I wasn't too convinced myself.

Uganda is populated by a wide range of tribes, some being ethnically different from others. A police unit often has members of several different tribes represented in its ranks. Few constables spoke English and probably did not speak any of the other tribal languages. Swahili was the lingua franca. Swahili is the language of the coastal people of East Africa and is a beautiful, but complex language. By the time it had travelled many hundreds of miles up-country from the coast, it had been reduced to an ungrammatical language which was incapable of expressing any subtleties. However, with typical government thinking newly appointed police inspectors had to pass a formal Swahili examination – written and oral – within their first two years to qualify for their appointments to be confirmed. *And this had to be pure coastal Swahili.* The only teachers were in Kampala, so it was just hard luck if you were stationed up-country.

One of my friends spoke fluent up-country Swahili, which all his policemen understood, but he just couldn't manage the coastal variety. He was now on his last chance. Failure in the oral exam, and his appointment would not be confirmed. He had been posted to Karamoja, a very remote area bordering the Sudan. Tribal dress was basic – not much other than 2 spears and a shield and nose and lip plugs. A language examiner – a Comoran Arab, who had originally come from an island off the East African coast – was sent by Land Rover to carry out the oral exam. On the way he ran into difficulties. Some of these had to do with the poor quality of the dirt roads, but the more severe were with tribesmen who were embarking on raids to take the cattle off the Karasuk people. They didn't like outsiders getting in their way. Fearful for his life, his mastery of beautiful grammatical Swahili was of no use whatsoever. He arrived at the Karamoja District Police Station, found my friend, and without hearing a word of Swahili, gave him a hand-written note to say he had passed his oral exam. Thereupon he returned as fast as he could to Kampala.

An appointment in the Uganda Police provided opportunities the like of which no constable would have in the UK. In my first year I was given the task of setting up a 999 radio patrol car scheme in Kampala, the country's main city. Being an observer in a Wolseley patrol car, in Hertfordshire once every 6 weeks or so, hardly seemed to be the depth of experience required for such a task, but somehow it all worked out well.

In early 1952, I was sharing a flat in Kampala with two other police inspectors. In the early evening of a stormy day, there was a knock on our door and we found an Assistant Commissioner of Police was standing there.

"Get over to Entebbe fast!" he ordered. "You are to guard the Queen's plane until she flies out."

Having no radio we knew nothing of the death of King George VI and that this was the first night of the reign of Queen Elizabeth. With the king very ill, she and Prince Philip were deputising for his state visit to Australasia. They were breaking their outward journey by staying at Treetops hotel in a game park in Kenya. Her plane had been retained at Entebbe airport in Uganda, against the emergency of the king's death.

The three of us stood under the body of the plane for several hours, shivering as a foul storm blew off neighbouring Lake Victoria, until it abated sufficiently for take off, two hours behind schedule.

Not long after that, I was detailed to form the first Railway Police unit in Uganda. East African Railways and Harbours line ran from Mombasa on the Kenyan coast to Kampala, a journey of some 850 miles or so. Railway Police had been in existence in Kenya for a long time, so a visit to them gave enough grounding to get on with the job in Uganda.

In 1952, a new Governor – Sir Andrew Cohen – was appointed, with the remit of preparing Uganda for independence in 30 years time. Independence actually came, unbelievably, in 1962. Although much work had already been done to prepare Ugandans for senior positions in all government departments, 10 years was not long enough. It was, so many of us thought, immoral to withdraw so quickly. The monstrous atrocities of Idi Amin can be attributed to this.

If you would like to know more about this period you will find Andrew Stuart's lively book 'Of Cargoes, Colonies and Kings' gives an excellent picture. It was published in 2001 by the Radcliffe Press, Oxford. Andrew was the son of the Anglican Archbishop of Uganda. He was brought up in African villages, speaking the Luganda language as fluently as a local person, and his love of the country is to be found on every page.

A LATE SUMMER EVENING

Our Creative Writing tutor, Sally Spedding, gave us the title, saying, "see what you can do with this." It seems a suitable story to end this anthology.

So quiet an evening. So still. No sigh of wind, no movement of the trees, their leaves crisped before time from want of rain, a gentle warmth still hanging on the quiet air. A lark soars high above the field, a speck hovering before dusk closes in. It drops so lightly, its trill proclaiming the pleasure of being alive and free to sing its song.

The summer's passing, September lingers round the corner. The farmer had stopped short of finishing the field that evening, the harvester and thresher parked alongside the hedgerow with all the other tools. The rest of the crop can wait for tomorrow. The wheat still standing, graceful in its bearing, luxuriant, burnished gold by the long summer's sun, distances itself from the rough stubble, where its kin had once stood, shoulder to shoulder, ear to ear.

Hand in hand, they walk up the hill towards the field, his jacket over one shoulder, her bag swinging from her unheld hand. They move in harmony, each oblivious how the steps are in time with the other, her calf length 'New Look' skirt swinging as her body moves.

The sun is tucking itself behind the horizon, spreading its colours across the milky blue of the sky. The wheat collects the last rays, the tops of the ripened heads now red gold, shadows darkening the stalks. They have reached the fringe of grass beside the field in that strip that separates the corn from the hedgerow, where blackberries are plump, waiting for the jam and jelly makers.

He spreads his jacket on the grass, bends and pats it into place, an invitation. She sits, then stretches out her legs towards the corn and smooths her skirt, turning to smile her thanks.

Seventeen. In their eyes, they are that much older now, with the summer nearly gone and school an age behind them. He stands beside her, looking down. Her eyes say, I want you here beside me, here in the glow that is all that remains of the day.

The lark has nested. From where they sit, holding each other close in the dusk turning to dark, neither of them sees the rabbits sneaking from the sanctuary of the wheat stalks to the exposed reaches of the stubble, gleaning the corn scattered by the harvesters. Nor does the faded blue of the cornflowers that edge the field catch their attention any longer.

In the late summer evening of his life, he is still walking up the hill, over the tunnel meadow, past the ventilation shaft that smells of the coal smoke from the railway below, onwards towards that corn field. Remembering the happenings of yesterday, last week, last month is an effort, but he can recall the detail of that jacket even now. But that doesn't matter as much as the memory of the colours of her skirt and its pattern, the slender waist. They are all as clear in his mind as they were that late summer evening.

His summer has long passed its time. Is this still his

autumn, or is life's winter beginning to claim him? Yet that evening remains as vibrant, these sixty and more years on. Stirring one memory stirs more but even the uncomfortable embarrassing remembrance of his youthful callowness, rising to the surface and painting itself into the picture after all these years, cannot take away the glow.

If you have enjoyed this collection of short stories, please try and find time to write a short review of it on Amazon.

ABOUT THE AUTHOR

Peter Wynn Norris cut his writing teeth on articles for journals, then short stories. His experience as a police officer both in Uganda and in the UK is apparent in some of these, as it is in his two novels, 'A Quiet Night at Entebbe' and 'Iron Snake'. Both novels were short-listed for the Crime Writers Association's 'Debut Dagger', an open competition for new authors. He is shortly publishing a book for children. He is a member of Northants Authors.

BY THE SAME AUTHOR

A QUIET NIGHT AT ENTEBBE

It is 1952 and the 'Winds of Change' are beginning to blow. African nationalism is gaining strength – unrest and rebellion are in the air. The unscheduled refuelling of the new young Queen's plane at Entebbe airport presents a perfect opportunity for a lone assassin.

Rosemary faces her own 'Winds of Change'. Has she lived too long in the shadow of her District Commissioner husband? Is it time to assert her own independence? With the help of Flora, an outcast 'soul stealing' sculptress, Rosemary's life begins to take a new path – a route that leads straight to the would-be royal assassin.

IRON SNAKE

It is the 1950's in a British East African territory. Africans still call the Railway "Nyoka wa Chuma" – Swahili for Iron Snake.

Luka Wamala, the son of a local chief, lays the blame for the death of his mother on the Railway Authority. He takes his vengeance through theft of goods on a large scale from railway wagons, knowing the Railway's systems so well that they are unable to determine where the thefts are taking place. Inspector Paul Carver is given the task of stopping Luka. With Independence imminent Luka is given unlimited power by the President-to-be. How can he use this to level the score with Carver?

20216872R00080

Printed in Great Britain
by Amazon